into the silence

into the silence

the fishing story

america hart

RED HEN PRESS | *Pasadena, CA*

Book design and layout by Jaimie Evans
Cover design by Mark E. Cull

Library of Congress Cataloging-in-Publication Data

Hart, America.
into the silence : the fishing story / America Hart.
    pages cm
  ISBN 978-1-59709-540-2 (paperback)
  I. Title.
  PS3608.A78394I58 2014
  813'.54—dc23

                        2014019057

The Los Angeles County Arts Commission, the National Endowment
for the Arts, the Pasadena Arts & Culture Commission and the City of
Pasadena Cultural Affairs Division, Sony Pictures Entertainment, and
the Los Angeles Department of Cultural Affairs partially support Red
Hen Press.

First Edition
Published by Red Hen Press
www.redhen.org

a c k n o w l e d g m e n t s

I would like to thank the entire team at Red Hen Press including Billy Goldstein, Crystal Gehr, Sam Haney, Gabi Morales and Becky Fink for being so helpful along the way. My thanks especially to publishers Mark Cull and Kate Gale: Every new writer is a risk and I'm grateful to Red Hen for taking a risk on me.

Thanks to my teachers: in piano, Doris Pridonoff Lehnert, and in creative writing and literature, the late Ed Dorn; Sidney Goldfarb, John Graham, Marilyn Krysl, Peter Michelson, Steve Katz, Kelly Hurley, and also Jennifer Dunbar Dorn and Janet Hard, all at the University of Colorado-Boulder. Also Manthia Diawara at New York University for his interest in my creative work, and Professor Graham Furniss, OBE; Professor Michel Hockx; and Professor Stephen Chan, OBE, at SOAS, University of London. Finally, at Pineapple Dance Studios in London, my street locking teacher Jimmy Williams, who has been an inspiration to me for years.

Thanks also to the Rocky Mountain Women's Institute and Bin Ramke for supporting my writing with studio space and a stipend for one year, and to the University of Colorado-Boulder for a fellowship and support through the Jovanovich Award. Thanks to the editors of *Black Ice* for publishing an excerpt of this novel.

I'm grateful to William A. Robinson, MD, PhD, and George Mathai, MD, of the University of Colorado Denver School of Medicine, for their faith and care.

Thanks to my family who contributed to the making of this story: My parents Charlene and Walt Hart, and my brothers Roger and David

Hart. Also my uncle Robert Neill Hart and my cousins Jamie Hart and the late Carol Ann Hart, as well as my late grandfathers Walter G. Hart and Charles Crouch. The newest addition, Nikki Janan Hart, was born after the creation of Natalia—but she looks just like her.

The women in my family also contributed to the inspiration for this book: My great-great-grandmother on my father's side, America Vandalia Cotton; her daughter Bennie Dean Burnett Cowger, and my grandmother Meck Cowger Hart. And on my mother's side, my great-grandmother Claytie Stone, my grandmother Aline Stone Crouch, my aunt Mary Jo Crouch Boyd, and cousins Eleanor Clay Boyd Bryant and Mary Kate Boyd. An honorary mention to cousins Bill and Charles Boyd.

Thanks to Melody Lees in New York City and Ania Blaszczynski Rowan in Boulder for years of friendship. And special thanks to Ania for reading drafts of the manuscript and giving invaluable insights.

To my partner of many years in London, Seraphin Kamdem, who with unwavering faith saved the last pages of the manuscript to read from a published book on the shelf: There aren't enough words for my thanks.

This book is dedicated to my father, Walter G. Hart, Jr., who took us fishing as a family, and who has always encouraged me to write.

To My Dad, Walter G. Hart, Jr.

a memory, a future, a past; beyond the place where, in the meadow, a girl runs forever carrying her hat, pink ribbon tied tight around the brim; with a walking stick in hand, what is she thinking—where am I in this morass, this dark blend concocted on my skin—surfing beneath the water, or gazing far off, into the trees; does my brown hair wave down my back, can you see, dear reader, it rippling gently in the wind; and if you were me, would you pull your hat off your head, or down lower over your eyes? the straw weave to leave an impression if pressed too long against your palm; the ribbon fluttering in the wind, tall trees groan in the breeze, a sigh as I take down the pins from your hair, pull loose combs that once pushed and pressed, pointed into your scalp, look: a hatpin; or something once inanimate that now comes to life; a conversation, that voice. that voice that surrounds us, coming from a place in the blackness never seen; a voice deeper than the darkest surrounding currents, tra la la, I am gentle and young, as she walks gentle and young, on through the weeds. a starry night surrounding her, in the thick of a meadow, carrying a walking stick in hand; uninterrupted by the breezes that whistle through the trees, it is I, in the meadow, or it is you, taking my place, wondering why is it that your sister has cut her hair, as yours spills out from beneath the straw brim of your hat, so long.

standing on the bank of a river, natalia stands alone. casting his line into the water, natalia's father stands on the river bank beyond her, at some place obscured from her view so that she cannot see his face, his green waders; cannot envision him nor imagine what he is thinking or feeling as he walks along the river bank, beyond her somewhere. I cannot be pulled by the strength of these forces, she thinks, cannot lose myself to the tug of the current, the fight of the stream. casting her line across the river, into the branches the hook catches, on the bough of a pine tree; but she pulls the line back; yanks free the bubble that rises above her suspended on the wind; retrieves the line, whips up the hook from the leaves; it drops through the air with a light whistle, like the sound of the wind in the trees, as it falls downward and back into the stream. you are not so young, natalia reflects, just as she appraises her own reflection, contortions of dark hair outlining her face, dark eyes barely visible in the smooth pool, the shallow puddle that has formed in the rock beneath her feet. she speaks in a barely audible voice, watching the current carry her bubble downstream, until the length of the line catches and pulls it back, catches in the current; and she slowly reels in her line, the way that her father has taught her to do, not so young, she sings as she reels in her line, not so young, as the fish rise or float lazily below. not so young, not now; not at this time.

she looks up from where she stands, wishes she could see her father's reflection in the river below her—see his strong features, shape taking form through the trees. she wishes she had been left with her mother, to wander quietly through the woods, looking serene at the mountains and trees. her mother would be gathering flowers just now, she thinks, making garlands in the sun—is that what her mother would be doing right now? she wonders, slowly reeling the line in against the current, the bubble hovering over the waves. is her fly floating steady in the river? shades her eyes to see; then listens to the hollow echo, sound of footsteps coming down the trail; turns around to see her father there.

howdy, he says to her—she thinks, this his best camper's voice—howdy, stranger, as he approaches her on the bank. catching any fish over here?

no. natalia indicates the forsaken fly on the end of her line. I'm afraid nothing's happening here—only that I have been singing quietly to myself, she thinks, water running over her toes in the stream. cold and dark, the water. she remarks upon this to her father, hands on his hips as he stares stark into the trees. she will stare someday herself, like this. that is what she thinks, and wonders what her mother is doing now. careful not to let the line back too far, when you cast into the stream. walker's lip is bleeding; natalia hadn't noticed that before. you caught your lip, she remarks to him now, he dabs a handkerchief at his mouth, does it hurt? yes, a little bit—. your mother—, he starts to say; and looks off again, into the trees.

why doesn't she come with us, natalia thinks. is it because her mother prefers to be left behind. natalia will gather an array of flowers for her mother, she thinks, they will put these in a vase. still, her father stares into the trees; then, I am going back upstream. natalia stands, helpless and disappointed upon hearing his words. she is too young, she cannot walk the extent of the trail to camp by herself; she is too tired to stand here much longer by the stream. still, walker resumes his position much further up the bank; natalia sits down on her rock, but she doesn't begin to cry, instead watching the fly and bubble bobbing restlessly in the stream; anxiously, she pulls them out; looks closely into the pool as a drop of water falls, like a tear from her bubble and into the stream; into the pool, a drop of water that causes her reflection to shake, minutely, a fragment, just a little bit; and so she imagines a cool and tranquil time, exactly the feeling she has now in these woods, but herself in a long dress, dark tresses waving down her back; a white straw hat in her hand, feeling the current of the breeze that will caress and dry the tears on her face. gentle and young, she sings to herself, softly in the breeze. gentle and young, as she bathes her toes in the stream, tra la la, I am gentle and young. she wades out a bit, to where her reflection cannot be seen.

small minnows and trout swim below the surface, dart between her legs, above her feet. restlessly, she feels the sand of the river bottom shifting; watches the granules that rise up a bit, before she repositions herself further out, away from the bank. fronds of seaweed brush against her calves, the leaves slimy and cold, but pleasantly smooth to the touch. she loves the current cold against her legs; loves moving away from the rocky river bank over sand and rocks that feel sure beneath her feet. tra la la, she thinks, I could float away if I'd like. she examines the trout swimming around her, floating lazily near rocks lining the shore. their fins and gills flap in barely perceptible motion, and natalia finds certain fascination in this.

at last she wades back to the bank, sits looking up the trail to where walker must be now, casting his line into the stream as the sun is starting to set; natalia sees it bright orange against the green pine trees; she feels anxious to begin looking for flowers growing in the meadow, on the bank of the stream, that she can take to her mother at last; she is anxious that walker should finally appear to her on the trail; that she should finally hear his footsteps as he makes his approach. but walker likes waiting for the finality of dark and the sunset, she knows, so she sits on the rock and draws her toes through the sand, draws her legs up beneath her and thinks about the kinds and colors of flowers she will pick. thinks about her image, floating now steady in the pool, brown eyes and thick and brown, long wavy hair. she thinks about the fronds growing beneath the water, bending with the current of the stream.

—~~—

or a voice, under a fiery sun, an inconsequential moon, in this universe of aristotelian phrases and fine perfumes, drawing the tides where it will; between stars at night, no mere mirage, a presence that takes form and shape against logical sense, bound by these pages, dear reader, and not begun speaking to you yet: what do you think of? this silence that surrounds us, dear reader, on a moonlit night, does a percussive echoing of the fragments of our lives float gently in the stream, like fronds that bend and wave; can you tell me, what of the silence in these? in firm blocks across a page, a wall, a field, impossible to traverse; is a fragment then an aberration, or distraction, attempting to float away, until a rain comes down in a steady torrent, or waves on the ocean surface this presence again, a cumbersome ideal dressed in a long flowing gown.

—⁓—

without a pink frock on, natalia looks down at her dress. it is not that her hair is not long and flowing down her back in waves of dark brown; but she carries no walking stick to balance with, no straw hat sits perched upon her head, that would float lightly above her on the breeze, to be carried by the river current, to be blown off her head in some whimsical way; no pink ribbon is then tied around the brim, there is no light colored lace, doe's eyes beneath dark lashes; her eyes are more like the men's in her family: the dark eyes of walker, she has inherited these. she wears a cream-colored fishing vest, dark corduroy trousers, a flannel shirt and heavy hiking boots; gold hoops in her ears, and three copper bracelets on her arm, that jangle every time she casts, if she doesn't push them up her arm far enough. she cannot understand why her sister and mother have both cut their hair so short, as she has decided on growing hers longer every year.

walker has by now appeared once again on the trail, three large and fairly full grown trout in his creel, that they will clean, he says, once they get to camp. natalia grimaces, at the thought that she must help clean the fish. this is a distasteful task that she does not enjoy; nor does she enjoy eating the fish, two tasks, she knows, that will be relegated to her: she and walker will slit the cold fish bellies, driving the knife up under the skin; pulling out the entrails, and she can imagine now the feel of sharp teeth, the ripping sound, the soft entrails falling out; her father has shown her how to push her thumbnail against the large vein that lines the fishes' backs, how to push up against the bone; but she has not told walker how she feels about this—about the fish that will not be skinned until they eat them, until they have been thrown above the coals on the grate of their campfire. natalia prefers to eat brook trout, their pink succulent meat; but she doesn't enjoy the picking out of bones or, worse yet, sharp bones poking into her tongue or gums, beneath her teeth.

once, her sister nadine got a fish bone stuck down her throat, and so natalia is in some sense sorry that walker has caught the trout. but enough for a meal, and this will please her mother, she knows. so she picks up her fishing rod and creel to hike with walker back downhill, happy that the sun has not set, happy that she can still see by the light to pick flowers for her mother, that together they will set in a vase.

—m—

indefatigable and undefined, gesture as though to fall into a coma, turn twice on feet, on pointe, in a pirouette; mark the spaces clearly, the number of footsteps and distance between as, clear and unassuming, a gaze falls, off into the trees, a soft sigh, an attempt to construct a place of unimportance, understand the clear insignificance of glass; in a whirlwind, words like leaves fly up from the sidewalk, gusting into the air, lofting up before spinning back down, as on the waves of an ocean, a transparent past; words as though angels surf with wingtips, touching lightly on the crest of a wave, in a dream or above a crowded sidewalk, across a street, underneath an awning, pink and purple and green, or is it cameo, a performance, dancers shifting unconsciously to and fro in the wind, trees rooted to one spot that bend and sweep under the dim light of a street lamp, falls the light mist of rain, forms twist in one motion, carry me in your arms does one say, words falling from lips, silhouette, hair brushing against the sidewalk and scattering leaves that scratch across the pavement and will blow with each gust of wind, that brings the cool night air and carries with it these dancers who stand together wearing white shoes, across the street, hair falling across a face as a glance falls from the moon, and they glance across the silence, peering anxiously into the dark, gathering thoughts in the silence of this room, behind a dark lace curtain that cloaks and serves as a veil, impenetrable as the moon, inviolable to the touch that would command a cascade of raindrops streaking the surface of a cold windowpane at night.

—〰—

something in the way moss swirls across rocks, dried lichen, dried seaweed on a rock; careful not to fall in his olive green waders walker steps across. he is mindful of the hooks in his fishing vest; mindful not to break the bottles of salmon eggs he is carrying along; standing at the top of the mountain meadow, it is walker who looks down and he thinks, I can see clear to the bottom, into the depths of this icy pond; rocks covered with moss and lichen, green grass that grows and waves in the wind. from these things, among these things sit the old people in their fishing chairs; the woman in a green and white lawn chair, who sips thin-lipped sipping slowly at her tea; the two old men hold their fishing rods, sipping at their beer: they must be freezing by now, walker thinks, as he lopes along the trail; they are sitting in exactly the same position, the same place as when he and natalia this morning walked up the trail. or did only one of the men earlier have his legs crossed—walker can't exactly remember this. did the woman sit so placid and content, sipping at her tea, putting another worm on her hook—the woman gets up now to walk around her chair; opening up a tackle box, she wears a white cotton visor on her head. she has not taken her dark glasses off, round as two coke bottle glasses, impenetrable as the moon. the sun has started to go down behind the mountain where walker is, but it still shines brightly on the people below. the two men motionless in the director's chairs, one of them sipping his beer turns his head around. the woman has spoken to them. walker wonders what she has said, wonders from the silence that surrounds him on this mountaintop. wonders as he lopes down the trail at a faster pace, small rocks rolling beneath his feet; he carries his fishing equipment, three trout in his bag that they will clean when they get to the pond. he continues down the trail, wonders is natalia there? turns around to see; hears his footsteps against the rocks as he steps across, how they must sound to the fish swimming in the pool below. he cannot think too much about this: if he steps the wrong way, angles his foot just once on the moss that lines this rock, he will slip and fall down, hit his head, break the boxes in which he carries hooks and flies, a bottle of salmon eggs. he cannot be too careful, walker thinks, as he turns around to look for natalia, to look for his daughter in the clearing where she gathers flowers, somewhere a bit off from the side of the trail.

natalia—. cups his hands to whistle, the signal he and his daughters give, when they are looking for one another on the trail. but there is no response; or is it only a woman who appears suddenly, close to him and wearing a long pink dress, a straw hat with ribbon bound around the brim; long hair falling down her back, from underneath her hat; does she carry a walking stick, hold flowers in the folds of her apron, to protect them from the light rain that has begun to fall down. shades his eyes to see—natalia, standing there shivering as walker thinks about the light mist that falls upon his daughter and himself; protected by their fishing caps and vests, natalia still feels cold as walker takes her by the hand, and she holds the flowers carefully, close to her body to protect them from the rain, thankful that she has worn long pants, since the evening has become cloudy and cool: earlier, the sun shone down warm, but now a light rain has begun to fall, cold against her shoulders and face; under the moonlight, because the sun has by now set, so that only soft rays of moonlight penetrate through the branches of trees standing high overhead.

—⁓—

or the shrill sound of someone singing in a rough-hewn voice, long whistling notes pitched high overhead, far above, in the trees. she continues gathering flowers, pink daisies and fern, as her father paces quickly the trail; she numbers the footsteps marking the distance between them: ten strides of his, she thinks, equal to fifteen of hers. sounding above the echo of her father's footsteps, between the hollow sounds of his feet hitting the trail, is someone in the background, whistling or singing a tune; the sounds of jazz rhythms, over grass that waves in the wind; a bass drum or a voice that sounds through the mist.

natalia listens to the sound of rain in the trees, listens and thinks of raindrops as drops transformed into mist, rising high above the earth. listening to the sound of thunder, natalia can't understand why her parents can't believe in god: she is sure, herself, that some such being exists. god might be a man in the meadow never questioning his world; or someone pondering, silent and still; or someone who quakes at the sight of grass chafing roughly against her knees. she contemplates a waterfall and stains of grass on her knees, echoes that die in the hollow air; a chorus of birds as natalia looks at the moon under the quickening night, and pulls her bundle of flowers close. crossing a carpet of moss and pine needles, she looks at branches shielding her from the moonlight filtering down through the trees; the path sinks slightly beneath her feet, spongy soft ground; and when another crash of thunder comes, the sound binds her to the fear that leads her body, that leads her closer to her father, more swiftly now down the trail, toward the sound of her father's steps.

sister natalia she thinks she would be, if she were a nun; she would play on a pipe organ, or the piano, at church. natalia sees from the streets, from where she stands on cement steps, outside, stained glass windows of the churches she has never been inside; she feels sharply drawn to the beauty of hymns and the consoling ritual of mass. if she sits still too long, either fishing or in school, natalia can imagine herself in a headdress and black gown; sometimes, she surmises, she might become a sister, herself. natalia walks down the trail and thinks about this. cleaning the fish, when they stop at the pond, she thinks about catholicism and native american dances she has been learning at school; of her best friend lynda, how her hair snakes out behind her, as she plays maracas, dancing in a black leotard.

natalia cleans the fish, pulling at their mouths, ripping from the jaw downward, accustomed to the smooth ripping sound of their entrails pulling loose; throwing them up and away from her body, somewhere far off, high up into the trees, natalia imagines entrails just disappearing, dissipating, carried far off into the wind; then forming invisible particles: spirits vanishing to become one with the light mist that floats softly down, creating a blanket around her shoulders and hair. she imagines the sacrifice of fish to be something like this: each spirit, each fish, going off into the sky at right angles; but from her peripheral vision, sometimes, eyes loom above her glowing eerily green, yellow, and silver from their heads; dark night sky surrounding mere pinpoints of light; then from within the darkness, the shattering sound, pupils bursting forth, popping out from behind the confines of their irises, escaping into the darkness with a loud sound that echoes, explodes into a scream.

—⁓—

if her mother stays behind, it is to sweep the floor of the tent, with the force of a thousand men, a veritable army, pushing dust up and away, into the clear morning light; shades her eyes to see: the sun rising over the mountains, trees delineated against a background of lichen covered rock; mountains gradually shading from dark green to the barren timberline covered only with rock.

natalia's mother looks at the peaks in the morning, to decide which one she will climb; she sits with natalia's younger sister nadine, close to the fireside, nadine playing with a doll; she dresses and marches it through the dirt floor, stops it on the fire grate, says, i should have gone fishing, mom. how can you go fishing, nadine. you are still too young. nadine's mother shades her eyes against the sunlight, imagines natalia sitting, fishing by the brook, as she gazes at one of the mountaintops, covered with snow—she thinks, as she starts pulling wild strawberries from their plants, cutting and washing them, she and nadine will climb the peak, up through the meadow and trees; she looks at nadine, points, do you want to climb that one? nadine nods yes, puts down her doll; but you can take eleanor clay, that is her doll, along. nadine smiles and dries her eyes at this; she did not want to leave eleanor clay, her best friend, behind. we will gather flowers in the meadow, her mother says, as she is lacing up her shoes. nadine is wearing a skirt, i think you are going to scrape your knees. against the pointed branches; we'll be going over some rocks. nadine pouts a bit; but does not want to change into pants. it's easier this way, her mother says, and brings her a pair of shoes. easier to climb the mountainside, traversing the meadows, jumping over pools; nadine listens to her mother's explanation, listens and thinks about this. she wishes she had gone with her sister natalia, who gets up every morning when her father does; rises up before the sun comes up, dresses in trousers and waders, then follows her father out, to where their fishing vests are hooked on branches of pine trees, pockets holding boxes of neatly tied flies, bright metal fishing lures. don't you want to come along, natalia always asks, shaking her sister, not letting her rest. but nadine is younger, a baby, natalia thinks, and prefers not to come along; but to sleep a little later, like her mother does; to have breakfast cooked over the fire in the grate rather than eat something cold from her pocket, as she stands alone fishing, on the bank of a stream.

—∞—

anastasia lifts her skirts over flowers and weeds, white lace petticoat, black boots that lace up, a thousand hooks and eyes; anastasia ties them in the morning, then shades her eyes against the sun, hand beneath the broad hat brim that shields her face, protecting her white skin against the sun's bright, hot rays. not sure where she is now, but hoping she is not lost, she has strayed into a clearing, away from the trail she is so familiar with—tall trees surround her, grass blows in the wind; boulders and smaller rocks feel rough beneath her fingertips, the lichen that covers them crumbles at her touch.

she sits down and unlaces her black boots, pulls them off and from one shakes out a stone; stands up in stocking feet, stretches arms to the sky; then lies back down flat, arms above her head, lies there facing the sky, over the rock and head hanging down, hair falling around her shoulders, into the grass. the sun still sits high above her, not approaching the horizon yet; and even if the sun sets, she knows, a full moon will rise above—she will be able to find her way back to her home, she thinks, lying on the rock—places the hat down beside her, runs the smooth satin ribbon between her fingers and over her hand. the rock beneath her back feels hot from the sun beating down upon it; she lies letting the sun warm her face, and wishes she could stay in the meadow, that the dark night sky would never come.

she falls asleep and into a dream; something about the meadow; at nighttime she awakens, the full moon sits globular above her; she stretches then sits up, pulls on her boots and laces them up. she hopes her father will not be worried about her; her mother will be putting dinner on the table, as anastasia walks away from the clearing; she steps over rocks and grass as she searches solemnly for the trail, looking for signs she remembers, for the path that would lead her home through the dark.

she twirls the straw hat on the fingertips of one hand; picks up a walking stick and gazes up at the moon. if she whistled, putting two fingers between her teeth, she could create a sound, a signal sharp and hollow and long. she looks all around her but doesn't whistle; instead sings a song, the grass waving softly; then suddenly, she hears the sound of the stream. she hadn't thought of listening for it, through the sound of the pine trees, whippoorwills, insects, and grass blowing against the wind, the sound of the stream, running; she walks now much more quickly, placing her walking stick, or putting one hand on her head, to keep her hat from coming off; or she gathers flowers, wrapping them up in her white cotton apron to protect them from the mist that has lightly begun to fall, over her shoulders and on the branches of pine trees; until, at last, she comes back to the trail.

between the hollow echoes of her footsteps, can still be heard her strange song—she sings or whistles, a clear, melancholy tune; notes that rise against the cliff walls and then sound back, longer and more hollow as they bounce back through the trees. surely her parents will be wondering about her, she thinks, as she walks along. but the full moon has risen, opalescent above her, shafts of light penetrating, filtering down through the trees. she walks down the trail swiftly now; her long hair flows out, blown by the wind, and it will tangle, she knows; so she stops for a moment, tucks it under her hat.

her sister rebecca has cut her hair, but she refuses to cut hers; refuses the feel of the cold shears upon her neck; dreads the weight of her father's words, as she heard them falling upon rebecca, while she covered her ears: why have you cut your hair, he bellowed, rebuking her, not a question at all; and now, three days later, he still hasn't spoken a word to her. anastasia bundles her flowers closer, holds them tightly to her and hopes her father won't yell at her for this, getting lost in pure daylight on the trail. almost at the bottom of the path now, she can see her parents' house, windows lighted by candles, her mother has put them there—she turns once to look at the trail before reaching the house, looks up at the moon, before going inside.

her mother sits at the kitchen table cutting strawberries into a bowl, you've been gone too long, but anastasia shrugs and pulls off her hat, long hair falling down. i brought you flowers, she offers, from the meadow; can we put them in a vase. her mother rises up from the table, not so unhappy now: yes, she says, a small canning jar—anastasia searches in the cabinet; finds a clean jar and fills it with water; your father, anastasia's mother starts to say, has been looking for you—. rebecca comes into the kitchen, pops a strawberry in her mouth. we have been worried about you; anastasia thinks she does not look as good with short hair, and is glad that she hasn't cut hers: she would not like to look like her sister does, no hair falling down her back; but it is not right that their father will not speak to her; she walks into her bedroom and looks into the glass. pulls off her boots and the long cumbersome skirt, lies down on her bed, an arm resting on her forehead, the other on the bed by her side, as she looks across her room to the window, at the drops of rain that cover the glass, drops of rain snaking down the surface of a cold windowpane at night.

—⁓—

her mother accepts the bunch of flowers from natalia, accompanies her indoors to look for a canning jar—they fill a small jar with water and settle the flowers inside; then natalia takes her mother's hand to go outdoors, carrying plastic forks and knives, a stack of paper plates; her sister nadine sits with walker by the fireside now, poking the frying fish with a long, pointed stick. she wants to shout at nadine, annoyed that her sister appropriates to herself such rights with the fish: if it is true that she thinks about catholicism and native american rituals while she is cleaning the fish, it is also true that she cleaned them, herself. natalia covers her ears as she shrieks at her sister, don't do that, nadine! I caught them, and I cleaned them—; but hush, natalia, walker steps up from the rock he is sitting on, places one arm around her shoulders. he is partially smiling, natalia knows, so she shields her eyes with both hands. he has certainly not heard the screams, seen fish eyes stare with starlight pinpoint focus, fastening their gaze upon her before exploding and shattering, like shrapnel flying into the air, then floating softly down. mere particles in the wind? natalia can't decide, as she feels the cold drops of mist against her hair and face, wipes her eyes to look up at walker's expression now, but she cannot tell him about such visions; she doesn't know how to speak with him about this.

—⁊⁊—

timberland boots that lace up, a thousand hooks and eyes; natalia ties them before walking to school over a short dirt trail through a field of wheat; most of the children walk to school from her neighborhood; only recently has a yellow school bus with black stripes started making one stop, at the bottom corner of her street. but natalia prefers to walk, sometimes up the hill to where jonathan lives; to the top of the hill where steve watches from his window, they walk into his house, wait for him to arrive downstairs in the foyer, brushing his hair; he looks for his coat hung on a brass hook, for his socks and shoes among an array of five or six pairs of boots, lying in a corner, sometimes piled up neatly, or scattered about the floor; steven looks through his sisters' pile of clothes, looking for his shoes and socks, as natalia and jon wait, hands inside coat pockets, talking quietly, not to awaken the children upstairs.

this day, natalia steps outside into the sunshine, she and steve and jon traversing the lawn, a shortcut, over which lie a number of massive dog stools; today, jon and steve step adroitly, over and between piles; but just before they reach the end of the yard, natalia steps directly into a clump, why doesn't someone clean it up, she wonders, looking at the overgrown weeds, unpruned trees, dry and brown, dying, cracking lawn. why doesn't someone take care of the yard, as she looks around for a branch, and tears one from a tree, a long pointed stick; she begins scraping the mess from her black and white polished shoes.

just the night before, she had finished polishing them: following her father's example, she had shaken a bottle of black liquid, brushed black polish on to cover the shoes; she had let the polish dry, then cut a small piece of cloth from a sheet; rubbing it against the surface of the shoes, she had attained a bright sheen. near the doorway of the living room she had left her shoes; she sat looking at her polishing job or out the window that night.

heels click against the pavement, jonathan and steven, too impatient to wait; while she sits still on the lawn, stench of dog turd filling her nostrils, making her sick, the two boys occasionally turn around, calling out her name, for her to come along. but she finishes scraping off the dog mess, takes off her shoes and rubs them firmly against the grass. now, her shoes will be covered with green stains; now, her polishing job will be gone. the school bell will ring soon, signal to her that ms. englebart will shake her painted nails at her, point at her as she comes in the school door and takes her place at her desk.

so she remembers now playing during recess the day before, on the bars, as the boys disappear over the hill wearing brightly colored jackets, that at recess they wrap around bars of the tall metal structure that rises up in squares: they push against the bar below for momentum, turning as they count, spinning, as many times as they can. or natalia climbs the bars, goes from hand to hand on the monkey rungs, spins and drops from the high bar standing a few feet above her head. from yesterday's games, a blister formed on her hand; her teacher had to tell her that's what it was. natalia had stayed in the cloak room crying, afraid to pull her sweater off; watching the white bubble that looked full to bursting on her hand, standing alone in the cloak room, until her teacher noticed her missing from the students lying on rest mats, terry cloth towels brought from their homes.

natalia never likes lying on the rest mats in the first place, she thinks, as she hears ms. englebart's shoes clicking quickly across the tiles, where is natalia, she is not resting; but napping, natalia thinks, is a waste of time: she is never tired at noon. and then ms. englebart is there, with natalia in the cloak room, she looks as though ready to shake her, to find out why she is crying so hard; she pulls natalia up from her position in the cloak room corner, natalia turns her face away and stretches out her hand. her teacher carefully pulls her sweater over her arms, over the blister, then hangs it on the rack, takes natalia's hand and says, it will probably stop hurting soon.

her mother makes natalia take naps at home, too, in the afternoon; when her mother closes the door, footsteps disappearing down the hall, natalia stands quiet on top of the mattress of her double brass frame bed, looks at the progression of construction, an apartment building down the street; a family that comes in a moving van, rolling over the black top when finally it is done; natalia sees them unload boxes, watches a young girl watching and sitting on the lawn.

ms. englebart's words are not much consolation, but in the morning her mother pops the blister and soon it stops hurting her.

the boys have by now disappeared over the hill, into the schoolyard, natalia hears the school bell clang as she finishes tying her shoes, and she wonders what the two boys will tell ms. englebart, if they will make fun of her, tell their teacher how clumsy she has been; and then, she sees her sister nadine, walking over the hill; the younger children begin classes later, so natalia waves to her sister and finishes the walk to school with her.

—◠◠—

from across a street, under a street lamp, misty glow in the rain; and gazing from behind glass, dear reader, or underneath a church window, or gazing up at the moon, from a sidewalk cafe, green awning overhead—peer through the cracks; sound of heels across white tiles; turning twice on feet, a pirouette; leaves in the wind, like the touching of hands or prating of feet across cement tiles lining the black pavement on both sides of this street for blocks, where cracks between the pavement form an abyss, water beneath a bridge, the still of a river current, deep and black; at the closing of eyes, clear and dark, imagine the woman sitting at her table, dark glasses, thick and dark concealing eyes; eyebrows that arch over and outline the upper circle of glasses perched upon the nose: is this the woman fishing, one and the same with the woman walker sees sitting between two men, fishing from the director's chairs? walker does not stop to ponder this, but continues his descent rapidly to the bottom of the hill.

and into the silence, now it is after the fact, like riding a bus to north point, to hawkes point, to another place in time; carried along smooth as a sailing ship, to another place not so fraught with memory, even as the mind is distracted by the pavement that disappears behind, underneath these wheels; think of a woman in a pink gown; a man in a fishing vest; think of walker and where he stands on the bank of a stream; a cabin in the woods, only a few hundred feet away—or is it a mile or two—it is hard to remember, thinking, standing here on the trail; to recall clearly a place, so much created in imagination: here, a cabin, there, a yellow and black painted frame house; a mailbox, a bed of roses, a house with shutters, white trim.

—⁂—

i am not one to walk so slowly down a hill, natalia thinks as she leaves her friends behind, talking about something, speaking almost as though in slow motion; natalia sees hands moving in explanatory gestures, watches feet slow as one stops to make an elaborate point and she hurries on ahead. they have made valentines for the school day, natalia's favorite a red large heart cut out of construction paper for nadine, large and folded in half, with a white lace doily glued on top—natalia had to be very careful about how and where she placed glue, smeared paste over the red. i love you nadine, written with black marking pen.

black leather boots that lace up, in the morning natalia had decided to wear these; the trail is muddy, she will have to scrape off her shoes when she gets home. carrying her violin in one hand, she goes to have her lessons once a week, tall thin violin instructor, black hair, he sings the melodies to her, asks is she counting the timing out; does she have her lesson memorized for today, the metronome clicking steady on top of the piano, a large black steinway grand that sits in front of the tall bay window; natalia wishes she could also play on this; and in a feverish state, because the only instrument she has is her violin, she carries the sound of the notes high and far and long, until they reach her sister's ear, nadine says, natalia, won't you ever put that thing down, walks by the living room covering her ears. i'm sick of you playing, she says, so loud. natalia can't understand why her sister thinks of nothing but her dress, how she looks to the other children at school.

natalia has explained to her sister the benefits of sleeping late, of throwing a boy's jacket on, she says, look, bends her elbow, shows her sister pockets for money and pencils: in one pocket she can carry money, pencils, and keys. nadine says, no one at school likes the way you look—natalia shrugs her shoulders, you don't look very attractive, natalia, doesn't anyone at school ever tell you that. they make fun of you in the lunchroom, you don't even know, the boys in the fourth grade; and natalia can't help cringing as her sister lists out the names, they point at you, would you ever go out with her; and they laugh at the way you walk, in your boots—and you are tall, natalia—

but in the mirror natalia examines her features quite closely, long and wavy and brown hair, not short and straight like nadine's; eyes brown and wide, her nose and mouth small; and as natalia's mother says, at least she has her violin; and her violin teacher tells her he likes the way she looks, her clothes, he says, suit her; but she wishes she were someone from another world, from a dream, when her sister nadine leaves the room, and she picks up her violin.

violin lessons, and when she goes and stares at the piano by the big bay window, one day, her teacher says to her, always staring, would you like to learn to play piano, too; but my mother can't afford it—; when, more than anything, she feels guilty, thinking how nadine will not approve, will say, i don't want to hear you play another instrument.

another instrument! nadine shouts at her mother and sister, says, i can barely study or have my friends over to talk as it is, points an accusing finger, the violin, she says, can be heard both upstairs and down. i can't understand why natalia wants to play yet another instrument. she says to her mother it isn't fair, natalia does whatever she wants, her mother asks nadine would you like to start again, maybe taking ballet lessons after school; but nadine says no, she is sick and tired of taking ballet, although it's been a year since she quit, natalia still takes ballet, and nadine is tired of it, she says, pushes her chair away from the table and in sliding almost topples back; natalia is afraid she will hit her head and so reaches out to break her fall, catches her and pulls her back; but nadine picks up her fork and plate, marches into the kitchen and natalia squirms, afraid the dishes will fly; her sister is good in school, she is pretty and yet, she sits at the table and complains; so natalia puzzles over her sister, alone with her mother and father now.

i think—, walker's voice breaks the silence, he sits with arms folded, staring out the window to someplace far off, at the mountains looming up behind the trees, as he pushes at the crumbs on his plate—and natalia thinks, it isn't that he's making much money now, putting floors in homes; or her mother, working in an office, natalia knows from the size of their house and her clothes, that her parents don't make much; but she doesn't have any idea how much, exactly, a piano costs—she could practice somewhere else—; natalia looks up as walker says this, and that way, she wouldn't be disturbing nadine.

nadine likes studying for school, her mother says, i don't understand why she is disturbed by natalia's playing, at all. i like to hear you play—; her mother gestures with one hand, and if nadine doesn't want to listen, she can always shut her door—; her mother and father begin picking up dishes; do you think you would mind

playing the piano at school, or in a church, at least until we find
out if you like playing at all; and natalia doesn't say she always has
wanted to sit inside a church, see the stained glass windows from
inside, she says, i wouldn't mind that, as she helps her father to
scrape the plates.

—❦—

she carries her hat, runs through the grass, now swinging the hat
against the wind that will catch and blow when the angle is just
right; she will turn, gaze at the trees, try to decipher the meaning of
the stream that flows beside her as she is running, swinging her hat
and carrying a long walking stick; the pink edges of her dress now
tainted with mud and water that has soaked through, the white lace
and edge of her hem drags, drags across the ground, water soaking
her socks, cold against her skin, as she walks on through the weeds
and she thinks, if ever someone should not have cut her hair—; but
it's a strange thing for a father not to speak to his daughter, even
when wondering why she cut her hair, when the length was so long,
that into the looking glass she would look, and see nothing else.
see nothing but the hair floating around her in the current of the
stream, where she so often went to bathe.

—❦—

natalia keeps a picture of her father's grandmother on the piano
when she plays, a black and white photograph; but her father tells
her the dress in the photo was once pink with light lace, and long;
her hair was like natalia's, only auburn, her father says, though he
doesn't remember her well, so natalia asks his mother, who tells
her she could play an instrument by ear; that when she was young,
always, her grandmother says, her hair was perfectly coifed and
combed, she stood neatly groomed in hats and long dresses, natalia
sees a picture of her in a photo album with a long skirt, wearing a
hat: your great-grandmother used to go hiking, her mother says
(one night was she gone so late, her parents feared she had disap-

peared somewhere far off into the woods; voices could be heard for miles about, her father worried and calling her, had she fallen, or gotten lost somewhere, did everyone worry, this time for good.

or was she merely walking alone, under a starry night with a full moon above, i will gather flowers for my mother, did she think to put them in a vase, a small jar, used for canning the vegetables that her mother made, like she made dresses, at home, she played the piano or sang, natalia's grandmother tells her this, that her mother would tell stories to her children, her grandmother says, just something she'd make up.

natalia asks her grandmother to tell her more stories, does she remember the ones that her mother told, but her grandmother shakes her head, says she doesn't remember much; but she remembers the way her mother played piano, when she was a girl, the hats and long dresses she would wear; and as natalia plays her scales she thinks about this, until she misses a note and it is not, she thinks to herself, simply that you sit down at the bench and suddenly know how to play.

her fingers have to be curved, her teacher has taught her how to press her fingers into the keys, with the metronome ticking, she plays a key and presses her finger firmly down; then plays the next key and presses and goes on like this, one hand at a time, and she begins with the left, fingers pressing firmly into the keys.

her teacher says her hands are right, that she is tall for her age and how her fingers reach a wide span, the curve of her hand over the keys is right, and her fingers are strong; but she should practice for an hour every day; by now, on violin, she practices for three: one hour before school, then two more at night. it's enough to make nadine scream, she knows, she listens to her sister complaining to her mother at night, can't natalia play somewhere else or do something else, but hush, she hears walker say, we are fortunate to have a child who enjoys playing violin, and one who enjoys studying, don't you have homework to do; but i can't concentrate, nadine says, when i'm listening to her play. you don't have to listen, her mother says, but nadine insists, natalia makes a lot of noise, as natalia plays at night, she overhears all of this, but nothing, she thinks, it is nothing, as she continues to play; then she reflects about turning twice on her feet, a pirouette in ballet class; but that is only an image in the surrounding silence until she hears the noise of a rough pounding, the beating of her heart; i am not so free, natalia thinks, at this time; chimes the church bell, or a clock, like sand filling a glass, click of fingers against a vase; the gentle drumming of rain on a glass; voice of a soundless scream or strains slipping through her fingers, like the sound of rain running down a windowpane, drops lying etched in stone.

or constructed in notes, three lines on a page, taps her fingers to a certain beat on a surface, turns in a pirouette on her feet, silently, arms outspread; standing on her feet as the moment stands still like a humming that fills the room; vibration of notes, like gulls' wings against the sun or a night sky, the notes natalia sings to herself when no music fills her ears. best to compose herself, natalia thinks, drying her tears or tying a fly; and if you have to follow a layout, a tie across two notes, or a line across the floor, natalia thinks, i'm not going to walk it, and puts her notebook down. in the isolation of a room, natalia thinks of anastasia, her great-grandmother dressed in long skirts; and her sister nadine, that together they will go buy flowers and put them in a vase: long stem roses, or orchids; natalia can't decide, as she hears the voice of her violin teacher, he says your notes have not begun to sing yet. you'll have to work harder than that. thick leather violin case, red velvet casing and gold buckles, two percussive sounds as natalia snaps her violin case shut. so what, she begins thinking to herself; so what if i can't get it right, or her pirouette, balancing in ballet; and she thinks how easy things are for her sister nadine.

click of heels across white tiles, nadine with her math book in hand, coming down the hall. too much studying to do, she remarks to natalia, putting her books onto the coffee table, how'd your violin lesson go. natalia puts her violin and music books on a chair, a clash inside, nothing happening here, natalia says; only that i haven't been practicing enough. i've been practicing long and hard, she says, why, still, am i not good enough. and nadine says as natalia thinks, so you think you want to be like me. you think you want to be like walker, wading far out into a stream; or you want to be like mother, reaching your arms into the sky. what of the people surrounding us, natalia thinks; what of the silence cold and dark; the percussive echoing around her built to such a pitch, like flames that are fanned, or waves rocking against cliff rock on a beach, fallen fragments of moonlight falling; a glance to someone or someplace far off; is someone there, natalia wonders as her sister asks, as her father gazes into the trees. what is he looking for, natalia? and is anyone really there, behind the gaze, beyond the eyes; glasses shielding him and reflecting the light, like two coke bottle glasses, round as two coke bottles, impenetrable as the moon.

there are things i still don't know, natalia thinks, and someday i may be five hundred miles from home—then, will there be nothing but percussive notes meandering, and could i be anywhere at all, could i be anyone at all, writing down notes. cold and dark the water, natalia thinks, while walking across a bridge, a span of gold wire; she sees a gold dome and imagines she could be anywhere, she could be in another city, driving across a bridge; in a city, driving across pavement, a five-lane highway, barely able to turn to look, across the water, across the city; across two languages, english and french.

—ᴍ—

a moment of pondering, silent and still; or is it walker, standing on top of a hill, can you see, dear reader, him standing there hair blowing against the wind, as he looks far off into the distance, hands on his hips as he gazes into the trees. what of the silence in the meadow; what of a moment pondering, silent and still, is there something in the night, dear reader, something of the silence in the trees.

or is he only getting older, carrying his fishing equipment and wearing glasses that serve to shield his eyes against the sun. if you were him, would you pull your glasses off, lower them from your eyes; or gaze further away, into the trees—mark the distance between us, between where we stand looking now, and the distance to go, further still, down the trail.

—∿—

what—. i don't know the answer to that. nadine puts her math book down with a slam. you should act older now, natalia says. it's impossible, natalia thinks, to concentrate while you're here. she gazes at nadine's placid face, the reflection of herself in nadine's eyes that look so much like hers. natalia considers how there is no solution now, except to leave this problem, to leave this house behind: the emotional strain too much to bear—so she carries her violin out of the house, practices the piano in church, or in a room at school, where she can go in and shut the door, alone, without nadine protesting against her.

gazing at the stained glass windows, natalia decides to read the bible, so that she knows the stories behind the glass mosaics; knows the stories of god, and of jesus, cursing a fig tree before being betrayed to die on a cross. natalia thinks it a particular kind of poison, a dream wafting, written into a textbook, told in a particular way, natalia thinks, like history books written for school; is there truth, then, concealed in her great-grandmother's diaries; notes written scrupulously, in long hand, black feather pen across a page.

anastasia puts her diary down. shakes out her skirts and wanders outside; shades her eyes from the sun, pulls the brim of her hat over her forehead, further down over her eyes, before pulling it off, to let her hair blow in the breeze; shades her eyes to see: a robin singing overhead, somewhere in the trees, orange cluster of feathers, chest puffed out, filling up with air—with the sound of the wind blowing through the branches, anastasia dreams up a melancholy accompaniment, impossible to reproduce here—like drops of rain on a windowpane, or turns in the field, when she is gone, mere leaves in the wind—dried and blowing away, that crumble to the touch; or like a ribbon, soft and fraying, or colors exploding into a wood, green and lavender, brown and blue, the colors of anastasia's dress and the ribbon that her mother has woven into her hair; dark tresses that flow down her back, like her skirts that swirl about her, in the wind; or the thick sound of branches falling; tap of a woodpecker's beak hitting sharp against the bark of trees; or saplings that sway over rocks covered with lichen, by the cold pool where anastasia sits, unhooking the buttons of her dress and boots; wrapping her hair on top of her head, unlacing her corset to wade away from the bank, into the stream; guards her eyes against the sun; dropping her head beneath water, she can make out plants and fish in the blur of water rushing by; hears the rush of the river current; pulls the pins from her hair, soaps and washes it. if she holds, for a moment, quite still, she can see fish underwater, also holding very still: do their eyes look out and up at her, anastasia wonders, rinsing out her hair. but it is at the sound of water splashing, when she drops to rinse her hair in the stream, that the fish no longer float serene in the river current, swimming a little bit away.

anastasia walks out, following a fish through the current. if she reaches out, she could easily touch one—would it swim away from her then, dots of color, pink stripes, surfaced from the water—anastasia can see tender white of the fish belly, imagines it cool and soft to her touch; but she can't think too long about this; nor about her father, she has seen him clean the fish that he catches, as they wrestle in his hands, in the brook; until walker knocks them out against a rock, hitting their heads. he takes out a pocket knife, slits the fishes' bellies; anastasia asks, does it hurt them, but her father says no, or only for a little bit; as anastasia listens to her father, eyes focused on him, close to covering her ears, letting out a scream; but no one likes to kill them (does walker close his eyes and begin to cry, a tear that falls onto the soft ground, forming a puddle beneath his feet). anastasia looks up at her father, but she doesn't begin to cry; asks, are you still cleaning them—. yes—. then, i'm going back inside.

walker stands, hearing his daughter's words; cleaning the fish, he imagines casting a line into a stream; closes his eyes, imagines wading into the stream, feeling the current and rocks beneath his feet, or looking at the mountaintops, as natalia sits, placid and content, sitting alone, fishing, by herself. walker checks sometimes, to see natalia; comes pacing down the trail, wonders is natalia there—sees her dropping her bubble into the stream, drying off the fly on her line the way that he has taught her to do; he has shown her how to take a fish off a hook; hitting a fish, hard, on the head, causes natalia to shake, a bit; but she comes with him from the cabin under early morning light; they walk to where fishing vests hang, hooked up on a tree. natalia takes from a pocket her earrings and bracelets and puts them on; walker gives her a candy bar or sometimes makes pancakes over a fire on the grate: he and natalia stand together, warming themselves by the fire, and walker asks, natalia, are you warm enough, before they start up the trail. he points out the sights along the way; when walker goes, as he likes, to some obscure place far off in the woods, over rocks, he often carries her, lifting her up on his back, or over his shoulders and he steps, carefully across the marsh or rocks or a brook, i'm getting behind—; and so walker slows down or picks her up and carries her, high up in the mountain meadows, where they pick flowers for her mother, where she and walker catch the fish; they will cook them for dinner, after cleaning them; an unpleasant task, walker thinks; but natalia comes along, and together they catch and clean the fish before taking them back down the trail.

walker is in the mountain meadow now; looks up from where he is cleaning the fish, to see the old people, sitting, still sitting, solemn and quiet, fishing from the director's chairs. walker thinks, if he could speak to them, or the woman who appears in a long flowing gown, dark tresses waving softly down her back; in this mountain meadow, it is walker who stands, and he thinks to look at the smooth stones lining the bottom of this icy pond, no fish or plants growing here—turns around to see, natalia, cleaning a fish—holding it in her hands, a fish that walker puts into his creel, we can begin walking, now, downhill—; going over the rocks, do you want something else for dinner? he asks, something besides fish. natalia shrugs. then, i'm not sure there's enough for everyone. walker says, if you'd rather not have fish, we can make you some vegetables, or something from a can, walker turns around to look, to see his daughter coming down the trail. doesn't make much difference to me—. you don't mind picking out the bones? no, not much—. sometimes, when i come by to see if you are still fishing, walker says, i see you, sitting there, sometimes singing—. natalia stops. and you are only singing—. i thought no one heard me, at all; i didn't know you did, i never noticed you—; but even when you were small, i would walk to where you were sitting, and wonder why you weren't fishing, but singing by the brook. just tired, sometimes, and i like to sing. your violin pieces? sometimes—. what did you sing before you played violin? just notes—

like the brook makes, or the birds; sound of the wind in the trees, the sad song of a woman standing in the meadow alone, wiping with an apron her hands, singing, clear strident notes in the trees; a woman, singing clear and hollow and long; does she wear a long pink dress, dark skin and black hair tied in a knot on top of her head. these voices in the mountain meadow could be god thinking in thoughts silent and clear, or the heavy sound of water running; the trees blowing high overhead, or clouds across the sky—

walker says, i wonder what nadine and your mother are doing now—. nadine's reading right now, natalia says, novels—. then, she's giving up on math? you can only work on problems like that, from a textbook, for so long—. but some people do. not nadine; she's getting tired of it. she wants me to begin reading—natalia sighs, as she reels off the list of names. does that interest you—. no—. it might, but i have to spend too much time on piano and violin. there isn't even time for all that. then, i'm going to play in an orchestra; and i want to compose music, besides—. walker stops. but i'm not sure how to do that, how to write down the notes—

the voice of someone singing, a percussive echoing sound; feet hitting against the trail, feet, and the sound echoes against the cliffs rising up, over the sound of the breeze that comes like a shrill whistling, the sound of the stream, and notes, someone singing; i want to learn to write all the notes down. a tie, the right rhythm where it goes; clear as that woman sitting and fishing, wearing a hat—walker looks at her standing behind him, at eye level even though she is shorter, because she stands uphill from where he stands, just a little higher on the trail.

suppose you could begin doing that, he says—you know the notes that you hear—. yes, but it gets more complicated than that, the number of notes, the sounds that i hear—. rhythms—. she shrugs; feels a bit hopeless, standing on the trail. then, walker says, compose one line at a time—. no, i hear complicated things—. then, start working on two or three. any melody you like, he suggests—anything, from the sounds that you hear—turns around to see her, drying her eyes; tears or mist? too complicated, she insists— but, we haven't picked flowers yet, for your mother and nadine—so together they gather a bunch, to arrange in a vase: pink and purple, an array of white. a woman's voice, the whistling sound of a flute; percussive echo of her father's footsteps, or the thunder sounding overhead. holds her flowers away from the rain, the rain that begins to fall as she and walker walk together, down the trail, past the clearing in the meadow, to where nadine and her mother sit, waiting for them.

you haven't been gone long—. no, walker says. then, natalia helped clean the fish. i don't think nadine should get to eat them; she didn't help. hush. i've been reading a book, natalia—; nadine stands up from her rock. i've been composing in the meadow; i'm trying to remember, so i can write down the notes—. what—another one of your songs? but walker says, she told me how she's going to put the notes together. you didn't help to clean the fish. i washed vegetables—. there may not be enough fish—. now, you want a fish, natalia; i thought you didn't like fish. walker looks at nadine, why don't you help cook the fish over the grate of the campfire. yes—and don't poke at them with a stick. i'm going to help mother gather wood. don't, natalia says to nadine, drop the fish, into the dirt—; or poke at them, on the fire.

natalia turns and is gone, among the moss covered trees, the damp smelling forest, and she can smell the fish from walker's creel, the burning of the fire, as she walks away from camp, as she and her mother continue gathering wood.

drinking a bottle of coke from a straw, shared demise; an image that will fade like glass that stands still on a table holding cut flowers, or a dress that blows in the wind, drops of rain, pieces of glass fallen, broken from the moon; a tie across two notes, the sound of a violin note that goes on and then is gone; notes of a violin, high up in the air as natalia looks up at her sister, i thought you wanted to become a concert violinist, natalia's mother says; i've been dividing my time, between piano and violin; how will you make a living, asks nadine. performing in chamber concerts; i can teach or play for the orchestra. and write at night. natalia looks at the photograph of her grandmother on top of the piano, as rain falls, drops clinging to the window glass outside, falling on the peonies and carnations that their mother has planted; sound of tires over pavement, walker back from work; natalia and nadine walk into the kitchen, listen: b-flat and e—notes of the refrigerator, sounds from the wires—

walker and their mother stop their conversation, your great-grandmother, walker says, could pick a song out from the radio—; he places forks and plates on the table, notes from the clock chime, natalia asks, did she write the notes down—in the confines of her desk, locked up after she finished writing, after brushing out her hair, weighing heavy down her back; a man in the meadow never listening to her words, or a woman standing in a long dress, wiping with her apron her hands, holding no flowers, a woman with dark skin, a voice silent and still; natalia, turning to walk down a trail, holding her fishing rod in hand when no moonlight shines down, wearing a long dress, a fishing cap, or three copper bracelets on her arm that create a sound to accompany the raindrops falling from the sky against a clear window glass; a soft wind moving through the trees, the silence about to turn on feet, count the leaves in the wind, pirouette; clear and dark, the water, the trees; hands of a clock turning, across the center until the shatter of glass and there you stand, under the misty night, glow of dust or light rain, a star bursting into gold and white, a flame, iridescent; across this sidewalk comes the light tread of footsteps on a stair, a cautious whisper stirring, barely audible, like the whir of two clock hands spinning, reflecting silence through a chapel window, gold and red, indigo, black; a walking stick, or a cane, a hat, indigo ribbon bound around the rim; along the bank of a river comes the shrill sound of someone calling, singing from a long way off—something about the way the hat is bound by ribbon, hair flowing out beneath a hat; walking among the trees, gazing at a starry night, further into the trees—a girl who cut her hair, when the length was so long that she would get headaches when she pinned her hair up on her head— walking through the woods on a starry night, the full moon above, someone worried and wondering, calling out her name.

—⁊⁊⁊—

white t-shirt, black tights, a black leotard; natalia watches the dancers getting ready for ballet class in the high school auditorium, stretching legs over the bar and arms over their heads; across the floor, arms thrown out, turning, natalia sees their reflections in the glass, they turn across the floor, then watch the other dancers, until their turn is up again; natalia watches as a new student takes his turn; after school, already there before class begins, natalia watches him, standing in the doorway; then, you noticed him—. he moved here over a month ago, i've already talked to him, dan is in my science class—nadine informs natalia; outside, leaves blow in the wind; falling from a cloudburst, drops, or mist—gazing at her expression in the mirror, looking at natalia, nadine says, we're going somewhere together, tonight—

hair falling around a face, a glance at her sister as she gazes into the glass; shadow across the wood floor, silence falling as nadine combs her hair in the mirror, he's a year older than you—and he's been invited to dance with some company, nadine says, so he's leaving—in a year and a half. a short black skirt and red sweater, white lace tights and black leather shoes, nadine, is that a new outfit? natalia looks up at the night sky, through the windowpanes, listens to the wind through the trees; pulling on the tights and sweater, nadine looks into the glass; natalia stands up from the bed, throws her jacket on. where are you going, natalia? i'm going for a walk—

looking at the river below, natalia thinks god might be reshaping her life in the present and past, or god might change her future for good, as a torrent of rain begins to fall, erasing her thoughts with the dust that hovers in the air; natalia dries her eyes on her sleeve and gazes at the dark night sky above, lies on her back, on the flat ground high above the river, sand and rocks below; until she hears the sound of thunder, like ocean waves rising and receding, the crash of water against a shore; the sound of rain in the leaves, rain coming down, cold through her jacket and shirt. she closes her eyes: a bird whistling overhead, far above, in the trees; light but sharp staccato sounds, drums and timpani or maracas, she thinks, shrill sound of a flute accompanying the percussion instruments; a simple melody, echo of rain in the trees, or the sound of water hitting against a shore; as she walks down the hill from the field she thinks to play it on the piano, to sound the whole piece out, on the piano at home—but then changes her mind, walking in the direction of the church. it's almost midnight—but she pulls at the brass handle of the door, opens it and walks down the red plush carpet that sinks under her feet like sponge, as she walks without making a sound.

light from the street lamps filters through the glass windows, casting crooked patterns across the carved surfaces, the church dark and quiet, candles burning on the altar, red velvet seats; shimmering in the candlelight, the black grand piano; natalia takes her jacket off and hangs it over the piano bench. she plays

a bach fugue, then ravel, music like water falling; erik satie, she
thinks, a repetition of themes; gymnopédies, notes slow and held
long; slow pieces, ravel; bass notes of a church bell striking; bach,
chopin, she plays through a nocturne; her teacher has offered to let
her practice in her home now, because of nadine; natalia arrives in
the mid-afternoon, after school, as her teacher works in the yard
or reads by the light of a lamp, i can't help listening, when i'm
reading a book—she shows natalia an exercise that natalia already
knows, one for the right hand, and another for the left. you have
to play the pieces slowly, you can't just play them out—; and natalia thinks, i'd rather listen, then—as she looks out the window at
rain streaking the surfaces of the stained glass, running down the
windows, in lines down the cross; she thinks of her grandmother
and anastasia, looks at the pulpit and up at the moon, her gaze falls
across the window, out beyond the glass—

as she stands looking through her notes at school, natalia sees
nadine shut her locker across the hall; then she is gone with her
friends, as natalia stands alone, staring after her. opens her locker
up, throws her books down; dan, coming down the hall, everyone
else is in class; nadine, he says, will take notes. i'm going to the
art museum, do you have a car? we can walk, it isn't that far—.
walking out the door and natalia feels the wind through her hair
as she and dan walk down the sidewalk; what do your parents say,
dan asks, aren't you always missing school—. but i don't always,
she says, i go to my piano teacher's house to practice sometimes—
because of nadine, she hates hearing me play—yes, dan says, look:
a snake crawling up the stairs, an anselm kiefer painting, straw
thrown against the land, books charred and fraying, set out in a
line; a snake across stairs, between heaven and earth, natalia looks
at this painting until she notices dan standing close behind; a
hand on her waist, lips against her hair, natalia moves to the next
picture, as dan takes a step back and natalia goes down the stairs,
hasn't nadine been seeing someone new? i don't know, natalia says,
she doesn't tell me much—

leaves in the wind across the church yard blowing, hands
through hair like leaves across the lawn, or the sound of water fall-

ing; the reflection of herself, or nadine's face in the mirror, hands across a face, contour of lips, hands through hair, and no one is free of the past, natalia thinks, no one without a history, like cracks in the sidewalk as she walks across; at night, natalia looks out the window as walker opens her report card and the rain falls down on glass; nadine pulling on a sweater and tights, i'm going out to-night; how can you go out; but walker says, natalia, you should study harder, like your sister does—a glance to her, or somewhere off, away into the future, or off into the trees; pictures above the piano, notes that sound and are gone, strike of a harp's strings above a cacophony of voices that sound like waves hitting an ocean shore, a stream winding down a mountaintop, like a ribbon bound to a hat; nadine, natalia says, dan says you've been spending time with someone new—who? asks nadine; and natalia thinks she'll begin to cry; and then walker is in the doorway, arms folded across his chest, don't you both have homework to do—; but nadine picks up her books, the door slams, pictures shake, anastasia and their grandmother, the photographs that sit on natalia's and nadine's dresser—but natalia is used to practicing inside a church, i don't mind leaving the house, nadine. looking at the stained glass windows, a chorus from the church pew, sound of a river running, echo of rain against the glass, or coming down through the trees, notes on piano written as an accompaniment for flute, and another part for violin; when i'm alone, just sitting, i imagine—

words falling from lips, hands through hair, natalia asks, what about nadine? dan says, we were friends. standing on pointe, turns across the floor; counting the rhythms out and natalia feels like covering her ears; across the floor; natalia looks at her face in the glass, long hair falling down; walker, standing in the doorway, you need to get some sleep.

walker standing in the doorway, it's past two o'clock, was the church door open, then? nadine says, natalia, he's going away— what did he say? natalia doesn't answer nadine now, as the notes disappear above her violin; dan's going to perform, and then be a choreographer—yes, but i'm writing music—my teacher says i could publish a piece, something not so ephemeral—where? in a children's book—oh, says nadine.

are you just getting back? yes. i thought you weren't awake—natalia, it's almost time for school, i heard your steps on the stairs; but i'd never tell walker or mother—not the details of it, no. not until after we leave home—what do you expect, nadine says—he's going away. natalia thinks, and i should go, far away, across the mountains and oceans—

why don't you go someplace else, her violin teacher asks, a city bigger than this—you could get a job in an orchestra—natalia stops to consider, and who would care where i go, walking across a bridge or dancing, gazing up at the moon; between pages, the notes between pages that sound nothing like the music she hears, in her dreams, in her sleep, sound of wind through the trees, clear and long notes, machines and cars passing, across the sidewalk, across the street; a plane in the night flying under the moon, the sound of pages turning, ravel, george crumb, paper clips over piano strings, stockhausen on a music box; playing jazz on piano or violin by ear, writing down notes, they convey my thoughts, nadine says; i like it, like the sound of water running—the sounds you said you hear—but you're only my sister, nadine.

thick leather suitcase, buckles shut tight; you could save enough money to come with me, teaching violin—i've been doing better in school. and what if i want to go to college—to study violin? natalia looks out the window, standing in dan's room. your parents don't mind if you stay—; natalia says, nadine is gone more than i am. always a different guy—; i don't know—i don't feel like talking about nadine, not now, when you're going to leave—

as dan gets dressed for ballet class, shoes in one hand, putting on his clothes, a bag thrown over his shoulder and he looks at the clock, then, i've got to go, i'm already late, as he slams the door going out; what are you going to do when he's gone? you aren't even spending time on violin. and look at dan, he always makes it to class, he spends more time dancing now, doesn't he? now, i have more time for violin. but you're always lying here, looking out the window—. i'm always hearing notes—; notes that you write down?

you better let him go—; he's already going, nadine—i know them better than you, i've spent a lot of time, with those guys—i thought you didn't know dan well, at all—but i did spend time with him— yes, i remember that; and nadine says, it wasn't to hurt you. i never guessed you'd get stuck on one person so long. you never get to know anyone, nadine, not really. why don't you get interested in anyone. i'm always going out with someone—. that's what i mean—

rain falling, a thousand drops into the grass; over the flowers growing, help me pick a bouquet for dan, roses or orchids, a bunch of flowers before he leaves, dried and blowing, vines that grow, honeysuckle climbing up a trellis, up to the sky; nadine helps natalia pick a bunch of flowers out, pink and purple, or orchids; a vase of roses, white and red; i never meant it, nadine says, pulling on her socks and lacing up her shoes, after dan is gone, alone, in a church or at a sidewalk cafe writing down notes that convey a melancholy sound, pages of music as days and months go by and natalia watches the dancers in the auditorium; it isn't the same, natalia says, lying on her bed; now that dan is gone, nadine asks, why are you missing school? to go downtown; a concert or the museum—i'm going to visit him, in december—; he won't have much time, now that he is dancing—

then, you'll have to earn the money yourself, walker says; teaching violin to children after school, small violins, notes that squawk and natalia feels like covering her ears, you have to practice harder than that, or listen to music; at night, in the confines of a room as nadine is leaving the house again, i think you should think about someone besides dan—there is no one else; but i can't, says natalia, think about leaving school or my family yet—in another city, i won't go camping in the woods—stepping over rocks and stones, natalia and walker carrying packs and fishing rods, is dan waiting for you—he still wants me to go. nadine says, you wouldn't be able to compose pieces from the sounds you'd hear—cars honking and airplanes overhead, machines clanking above the sidewalk, wind blowing paper like leaves, dried and blowing in the meadow where walker and natalia stop to fish, i don't like the feel of catching them, when they fight against the line—but we'll catch only enough for a meal—

are you going, then? yes—i can audition for music school, if i want to go back later on—and you should go to a conservatory, to perform; you should have a composition teacher, her violin teacher says; i'm not sure. theory and counterpoint—but then, i've never been good at that; playing by ear, jazz from records or the radio, sarah vaughan, nat king cole; five hours a day, two on piano and three on violin. if you really want to perform—; that's why i'm going away. if you had more friends here—; but i don't have time, nadine—now, dan has no time for you. that's why i'm going—

i wish i could go to another country, she says to walker, unlacing her hiking boots. how many trout? four; enough for a meal—; nadine and her mother stack paper and wood, light a fire, and throw the fish over the grate, as across the night sky, stars pierce through the black, creating points of focus beyond the tops of the trees; anastasia looks up at the constellations, look, rebecca—she points orion out, her hair hanging down to her waist, flowing from beneath her hat like the dresses she wears, blowing in the wind as she picks up a walking stick; you are the oldest, you should get married first—but there is no one, and i think i would know—yes, i did, rebecca says; then, he didn't even notice that i'd cut my hair—he thought i tucked it under my hat. but i wish it didn't have to be like that—i would rather teach in the boarding school—; a path that cuts through the trees where rebecca and anastasia bathe. anastasia pins her hair on her head—you don't get headaches, ever? no—. you are lucky then—to be able to leave school, nadine sighs. but i'm going on in violin. at least you have dan—i've seen him twice this spring—but he still cares for you—walker frowns, he cares about his dancing, don't you think? you could have gone on in ballet, natalia's mother says. i guess we'll never know—remember— when your friend lynda was dancing—. in a black leotard, spinning across the floor, long hair tied on her head—anyway, it's beside the point now—natalia stands up from her rock. was that enough fish? enough for me, nadine says, are you going in the morning again? five a.m.—walker sets his watch.

what will we do without you, nadine asks, who will catch fish? walker, won't you hate going fishing alone? but i'll be back in the summer, says natalia, i'm not going for good. her mother finishes her fish, throws the skeleton on the fire—i could stay there for a few weeks—you will like all the museums. and your only friends were in music class, nadine says, so you should feel right at home. i'm not going to one big music class, nadine. but there will be people with similar interests—natalia shrugs, it's getting dark—yes. add some wood to the fire, is there more? nadine can go get some. watch out for the bears—i'm not afraid, natalia. just think, you won't be able to see the mountains from where you are. i'll be back—but all the time you spent lying by the river, you'll never be able to do that, cities are all concrete—

across the parking lot, leaves dried and blowing, i don't want to leave now, dan says. nadine and i picked out a bunch of flowers; orchids and roses? we thought you'd like both; they're my favorite, white and red; i'm coming with you, nadine, wait. grab a flashlight—i've got one. do you have to use the outhouse? hurry up. it already smells, and it's only june. can you see? shine the beam down, not just in front of you—what did he say? about the flowers? he said they're his favorite—both of them, orchids and roses?

natalia sounds the notes out on her violin after dan is gone, or on the piano at church, at home, without nadine protesting against her—i'm sorry, natalia—; he is leaving, then, walking down the concourse; will you come with me? natalia dries her eyes, maybe you will do better in school—; and now i have more time for violin—composing music. hands pulling back her hair as he kisses her lips, i'll come to see you—my parents will be here—steps echoing down the aisle, a line of people and dan turns to look; natalia drying her eyes as he turns then is gone, mere leaves in the wind, flying above her, overhead, in the trees—

i didn't know you would miss him so much. why wouldn't i, nadine? i don't see why you can't find someone else. but who do you really like, how many people can you care about that way? nadine shrugs, i think you can like a lot of people, i guess. i always have a lot of friends. then, it's a matter of time—. but i do well in school, too. that's different from having to practice an instrument. she sighs. hold the light closer—we don't need much more wood—will it rain tonight? i don't think so, you can see the stars, the dipper—there.

where? natalia points out the configuration, the four stars of the la-
dle, the handle—see? yes, says nadine. enough for tonight? enough
wood? yes. we ought to be heading back, then—natalia says, i didn't
think you liked it out here—especially not at night. no—just because i stay with mother, to go hiking during the day—who's going
to go fishing with walker when i'm gone—you should learn how,
nadine, or at least go with him, sometimes. won't you be back by
summer? yes, maybe so—but if i'm not, you should keep him company. look. turn out the light. what? you can see everything—the
mushrooms growing here—can you eat them? no—. i'll learn how
to fish, maybe—but i hate the idea of cleaning them, pulling out
their guts, the sound of their insides coming loose makes me sick.
it's not so bad—and you like fish so much, if you don't go, walker
won't catch enough by himself. but if i clean them, i won't be able to
eat them—they'll taste different, i'll be thinking of their blood and
guts. oh, nadine. here, turn the flashlight on. are we lost? camp's
right over there. see the fire? i couldn't, through the trees—
    then, are you still missing dan? why wouldn't i be? i can't imagine
it, that's all. you should be more imaginative, nadine. what does it
have to do with that, that isn't the word that i meant. only that i have
never felt that way about anyone, ever. not dan? we were friends—i
think you get carried away. i get over relationships very quickly—.
that's because they never last long. where is the path? here—we're
taking a short-cut—are you sure you know where we're going? don't
worry, we're about twenty feet away from the campfire—listen, you
can hear walker's and mother's voices, now—beyond that rock?
give me the flashlight, you have to climb over it—what shoes are
you wearing? nadine starts climbing up the rock, natalia, i've gone
camping as long as you. i know, but you aren't very practical—are
you making it up to the top? how am i going to get down. you have to
jump, or slide across—there's a footstep to the left. did you fall? i'm
all right. sorry, we could have gone the other way—natalia? hurry
up, walker is calling us—nadine whistles back, over here—nadine?
he can't hear us, hurry up, or he'll go looking on the trail. can you
get over with the flashlight? yes—don't worry—we haven't been
gone long. you have the wood in your pack? of course—. i didn't see

you put it there, i thought you might have forgotten it. walker? over here—you two have been gone a while—not long, but it's dark—it's late, if we're going to get up at five.

—at five—rehearsal is at six, you'd better get up—you're going to be late for class—do you want to go? i can't take violin and practice piano—i thought you liked piano as much as violin, dan says. not really—or, i'm not good enough. i'd rather do something else. are you sure? if you quit now, you won't be able to start again, her teacher says, maybe you should keep taking lessons for a while—it's already too late—not to teach—there will be no time for violin—i want to compose music, and i'll teach violin, until i decide what else i want to do—but i'll still come here—; as the door shuts behind her and natalia walks away, a glance from the moon or someplace far away, gazing into the trees—walker? she asks. walker, is it raining? only a little bit. it doesn't make much difference, do you still want to go out? i'll make a fire—pancakes—and she and walker stand, warming themselves by the fire, it's getting cooler now—close to fall, a chill in the air as leaves turn and natalia walks across the churchyard—i'm definitely leaving school. you've decided for sure? with only a year to go—but i can make up the work—how much of this is because of dan? what does that matter—i've never liked being in school; walker offers her a hand, can you make it across?

i don't need help—i used to have to carry you, you know—i remember that, natalia says, walker? it isn't like i'm giving anything up—your grandmother, walker says, used to go fishing with us; when i was young, we would sit in chairs, like those people sitting, in the director's chairs. the woman, wearing dark glasses; instead of going hiking? yes—. i'll be in a city, and that's better than going to school—. but is it practical, nadine asks. a glance to someone or someplace far off, in the trees; in the meadow, her mother would go off into the woods, hiking alone—or with nadine, do you want to go fishing, walker asks. yes—then, you need to change your shoes— we're going to be going over some rocks, marshy ground—. i've gone hiking with mother, i know. you're planning to change, then? i guess. you're not going to make it, wearing those shoes—like a gift out of time wrapped around hair, a ribbon bound to a hat; beyond the glass, a plane flying overhead, stacks of music, notes written in the confines of a room; the church, or a white room at school; tread of footsteps on stairs; can't you get used to it, i'm doing the best thing—. you're too young to be going on your own—. your suitcase, natalia, is this all you're taking? the sound of wind in the trees; anastasia when she turns and is gone—walker, arms folded across his chest, or casting a line into a stream—but i'm not leaving for good—across the wires, notes of a violin; books from the library that nadine brings home to read, nadine says, natalia—

walker, staring across the dinner table as natalia fills out forms, reams of paper under the notes of her violin—i'm composing more pieces, listen—plays the melody on violin; an accompaniment on piano, above the violin, a flute—walker looks at her, but how will you make a living—writing down notes, across the miles, across the wires; a highway snaking into the distance under the rain that falls; wind blowing, across the sky, clouds that float above her, carried lightly on an ocean current, three notes, carried on a wave; as walker stares at her packing in her room, you said i would have to teach violin—and now, i'm teaching violin. she throws a sweater into her bag, i told you i was leaving last summer, fishing by the brook; singing notes to accompany the sound of the water rushing by; sounds on violin, in a motion, falling out of the night sky, an image of anastasia that fades and is gone; a picture on their dresser; walker, in the doorway, arms folded across his chest; does her mother begin to cry; walker says, we don't think you should leave; that's not what my violin teacher says, and i have the money to decide; a plane ticket, buckles shut tight; nadine shakes her head and whispers, how can you leave, and upset them like this? make good grades and be sure of getting into college then, natalia says. you're sure you're doing what you want? if you leave now, natalia, walker will miss you, i can't go fishing with him; in the fields, up the mountaintop, picking flowers growing by the stream—i can't, says nadine, take your place— walker, standing alone in a field, flowers blowing in the meadow as he sits on a rock, gazing at the sky now that natalia is gone; does he put his head in his hands and begin to cry, across a meadow—

natalia, wake up. you're going to miss your plane. will dan pick you up? yes—and you will be staying with him. across the pavement, someone in the meadow never questioning her world—across a wood floor, steps; you could have done more in high school, natalia—i'm leaving, nadine; here, i got you a book. natalia throws her clothes in a suitcase, shut tight, i'm leaving—until summer, at least. ripple of water across a lake, a breeze blowing the ribbon that anastasia has tied around her hat—hands through hair as she shakes loose pins, letting her hair blow against the breeze; lifting her blue cotton skirt to walk over weeds, alone, no one watching her, anastasia shakes out her hair, in the sun; not too long, she thinks as she slips a foot into the water, pulls up her skirts, and wades out a bit; she looks at the plants in the water, mud rising beneath her feet; sound of whippoorwills singing in the trees, a robin's call that sounds then is gone; light from the sun casts crooked shadows through the trees; the moss on rocks soft and spongy to her fingertips; she picks up the hat, runs the satin ribbon through her hands.

natalia picks up her violin. i'm going across the ocean—what? walker puts the book he is reading down. wherever this takes me, the sounds that i hear; the sad feeling of a woman standing alone, wearing a blue dress and holding her hat, twirling a walking stick under the sun that shines brightly down; dance music that swings, like the hair falling down her back as men pull her in turns across the floor, it doesn't sound like that—the sounds that i hear—a thirteen chord? her teacher asks. then, go to school, if you can't write down the notes.

across the meadow, traversing the fields, anastasia says to her father, i would rather teach at the boarding school. anastasia's mother looks at rebecca, at least one of our daughters, she says, will be married. but i don't want to live here—the boarding school is far away. maybe you'll meet someone there, rebecca says, you never know, how the timing will be; you might meet someone new—the sound of water hitting a shore; as the plane engines slow, a change of altitude as natalia's stomach sinks with the ocean waves, a river snaking between buildings rising high above the earth; the sound of tires screeching, glare above the runway as the plane slows and stops, pulling away from the windows where walker watches natalia now, does he cover his eyes, pull off his glasses to look—natalia, sitting by the brook, singing, alone—

i'm afraid of going, now, but don't tell walker that. natalia? you know how he feels—i'm afraid he'll convince me to stay; maybe i really don't want to go. you always talked about wanting to leave; even when you were young, you wanted to go out with walker, rather than stay home. but this is the place i know: a city, with mountains and trees—there will be more for you to do—besides, dan is there. i'm not sure i care about that now—natalia looks at her sister's face in the glass, cut flowers standing in a vase on a table beside a telephone; wood across a floor; sound of the plane engine that crescendos, natalia's suitcases packed and her violin in hand, walking down the concourse holding walker's hand; i won't be gone long, walker—

her mother wrings her hands; look at the stone on this—anastasia holds the ring in her hand, weighing heavy as the stones she picks up in the meadow, smooth and worn, cold to her touch; she gives rebecca back the ring; like the rocks where she goes to bathe, she thinks; she thinks of women sipping lemonade on the front porch of her grandmother's house, a cabin in the woods; logs stacked and burning on the fire; paper that natalia buys in the store, staff paper, green with black lines. i didn't know you thought about it so much, dan says. nadine told me that you do nothing, a lot of the time. lying on her bed or in the meadow, stepping across the pavement as the light turns and she walks, slowly, that's how you play this part. so quiet? and then it builds, to here; hands through hair, above her, rain; the sound of thunder in the night air as wings above the city loom beside the river; bow against violin strings, crash of waves against a shore; in the shade of a hot july summer, rain as it begins to pelt against a windowpane; leaves in a whirlwind, waves breaking against a shore under a night sky; stars billowing in a smoky light, irreplaceable as this woman sitting in the director's chair.

turn around, at the sight of a ribbon fraying, dust on a desktop where a diary sits, still on a desk with pictures now yellowed at the edges and fading, pages that crumble to the touch; at the turning of a page comes the sound of a shrill whistling, so that this woman looks around, getting up from the director's chair—what is this strange and sudden sound, quarter tones now, a swift melody like running feet down a trail, quarter tones sharp as a bow tapping against the wood of a violin, the collective ensemble that picks up their instruments to the strike of a baton; wheels screeching against a runway; it is walker, taking off dark glasses, it is the woman who turns around; an ensemble, clear as glass, frail as a china tea cup, the chime of a triangle; church bells after the clack of feet in black shoes across white tiles, cacophony of voices, women tuning instruments, above the rustle of pages like leaves, voiceless whisper of an audience descending into a theater with red velvet seats, hush above the gold trim, an opera glass, eyes focused on an audience collected in the auditorium, on stage under bright lights, feet tapping down a flight of steps; a plane slowing in the night, turning clockwise, in close toward the river, above an array of lights like the still points of stars, a thousand voices ringing out in the silence that is still above waiting to be felt, like a night breeze rustling through silk; velvet seats and a cone of light from a theater spotlight, white ties and black shirts or white dresses with sleeves that billow like angels' wings, a chorus waiting to be heard in clear notes down an aisle, above an audience, in an auditorium through the sound of whispering, notes, a silence long as the river winding through the mountaintops, or the sun's rays projecting through the trees as anastasia wraps her skirt around her knees, reading a book out loud; pages fraying, a line of notes that sounds through the hollows in the air, carried across the still of a river current, a woman whose sigh is barely audible, coming through the sound of silence, barely stirring, two maracas shaking, then the sound of timpani like ice that cracks and breaks above stream of notes, on violin, bows tapping, chorus of angels and instruments that produce a staccato sound, paper rustling, the piano melody, a single note above the percussion instruments sounding, paper clips on piano strings, striking of a harp, then percussion in-

struments, eighth notes as the piano begins a simple melody, a chorus of women in white robes, sleeves that hang like angels' wings
above the violins; screech of tires against pavement; a plane coming
to a stop, along the runway, blue lights point like stars, whir of engines that crescendos and then disappears, like lightning striking
to the pavement, a black runway disappearing beneath the wheels,
rain streaking a window like tears against a face, walker's face behind the glass, does he shake his head as natalia leaves, does he hold
her hand in his as he walks further up the trail, a starry night surrounding him—is he carrying a lamp—does he push his sleeves up,
lean down close to the water, where he can see his reflection in the
pond; gold rims of his glasses reflected as he leans and they make a
splash, then are carried by the river current, a little bit away, before
walker wades out to retrieve them; pulls them back before they begin to sink, pulled by the river current; but walker reaches out to
grab a rim, bending the frames minutely, a fragment, just a little
bit—he examines the frame of his glasses, gold surrounding glass,
before he wipes each side against his flannel shirt, smearing the
drops of water away and then readjusting them; sliding them over
his eyes again, he turns to see the old woman sitting alone, solemn
and quiet, fishing from the director's chair; standing at a podium,
conducting an orchestra, one clear and uncomplicated tune, like a
snake coiled beneath a staircase or a ribbon bound around a hat; soft
waves of moonlight fragmenting, the light that shines through the
trees where walker reads a letter; natalia, in the apartment where
she and dan live; a mattress on the floor and two framed pictures
above the bed; anastasia's photo on top of a piano; walker and his
mother; natalia, teaching, during the afternoons, and in a chamber
group, writing at night or practicing during the day, walker reads,
before placing his creel on the ground; as he pulls out two fish to
clean, natalia's mother says, it wouldn't have been long, before she
left—and we couldn't have convinced her to stay. but nadine kicks
at the dirt beneath her feet, sweat beading against her skin, in the
small apartment where natalia and dan live, a fan that blows against
venetian blinds, where natalia sits on the window sill; increased
heat in the intensity of a city where natalia collects notes like leaves,

blowing into a brook or across the sky, lights like pinpoints; across the sidewalk, steps, up the stairs—dan, turning the key in the lock, home late at night, as natalia practices on piano or violin, away from the mountains and trees where walker stands alone, casting his line into a brook—i wonder what walker is doing now; natalia looks out at the pavement below, neon lights glowing across the street; she pulls the window blind down, picks up her violin. what's that piece? just something i made up—a woman who finds herself alone, in a field, above a river, a plane flying overhead—i hear it with a chorus, women singing in robes, a harp, voices above percussion instruments and a light that shines down like a cone, focusing on the instruments below—did you write all this down?

leaving the theater, but it only comes every once in a while, through the silence, in sleep like a whisper that leaves, carried along on a bus or train, smooth as a sailing ship—cut pieces of glass falling, fragments broken from the moon, sounds that come like images through dreams, carried across an auditorium like steam over a cup of coffee as she and dan sit, as dan glances at the clock and he looks at natalia sitting across from him—i'm going to practice, then try to write down these notes—are you going to miss your chamber group? no—. as dan puts the dishes in the sink, natalia says, i never seem to get the right sounds; she gets up from the table, the right combination of notes, the silence at the right time, or the instruments i really want—what are you looking for? this piece, the one i was playing last night—do you have time to listen? you know how rehearsals are—natalia stands up from the pile of manuscripts strewn about the floor; and you should call that cellist—i don't have enough time, teaching and playing these instruments—pieces slipping through fingers, across the waves, into the ocean; where do they go? dan says, even if it's in the future; even if you have to wait— but what about the time spent waiting—did you call that cellist? playing weddings and bar mitzvahs; we're on for the summer—

the melody above percussion instruments, like a ribbon tied into a bow, across the mountains and trees, to the south, a train running—filling out forms; i thought you never wanted to go back to school—across the floor, turning; i just wanted you to tell me,

do you think the notes are right? on violin, a part for flute, i don't
know—i wish they could shut off that glaring light; glowing pink
across the street, sound of a radio blaring, natalia? it's only five
o'clock—i'm going to get up—i can't stand the sound of the music
in that apartment playing, and keep the window shade down—the
rhythm of the streetlights that are glaring, pink neon and blue,
from the movie theater—close the shutters—the lights across the
street—i don't mind, natalia says, i've grown used to them—walking on the sidewalk, beneath the moon, natalia waits, a breeze
carrying her as rain comes down and a train goes past, blowing
back her hair like a cool river current or a breeze underneath the
starlight where nadine sits with walker and their mother now, and
natalia picks her instrument up; nadine asks, she's auditioning in
violin? and she's playing in a trio—

as the nocturne plays and anastasia sits, a bouquet of flowers
thrown over a banister, a sigh as anastasia shades her eyes to see
against the sunlight; a gold ring on a finger, heavy as a weight of
lead; the rock where anastasia sits, a tear that falls, a flash of lightning fading in the night sky as anastasia lifts skirts over weeds,
carrying her book down the hill with a bouquet of flowers for her
mother, somewhere in the meadow; anastasia turns in the meadow,
or steps down an aisle, dressed in white; under a night sky, nadine
sitting by the fire, poking the frying fish with a stick; walker says,
you know how natalia would scream at you, if she saw you doing
that—yes, but she's gone now; a tear into the fire, smoldering at her
feet, coals hot and glowing, fragments that spark as nadine stirs
them until they are lit, bursting back into flame; the cautious stir
of a whisper floating; anastasia, in the trees; walker, taking a letter
from a pocket that he opens standing by the fire, words across a
page, natalia, walker says, is thinking of leaving—she's going? her
mother says, she may be going to move alone. because she spends
too much time teaching—. nadine says, walker, aren't you worried—because she didn't finish school. but she might get into music
school—i thought she wanted to compose music, by herself—what
is she going to play? bach; saint-saëns, germaine tailleferre—

neon lights glowing pink and reflecting off the windowpane, papers across the sidewalk, sand and dirt blowing; thousands of steps, up an aisle until anastasia arrives, at a podium, an orchestra under bright lights of an auditorium; a bridge, an abyss, someone praying against the dark in a white robe that enfolds her, rustle of silk as paper turns; a violin note over percussion instruments, nadine, we're going fishing now. do you want to go with walker? i don't mind—suitcase buckles shut tight; walker, leaning against the plate glass window as the plane begins to taxi away; whir of engines as natalia kisses dan good-bye, at the door of their apartment, is that all you've got? yes—your violin—your train ticket? yes—you might as well fly, natalia; but i'd rather take the train; sure you can't come? you know how rehearsals are—

white shoes across a cement walk, natalia walks carrying her violin; on note paper, her own lines, a treble clef; the timing isn't right—this part in three-eight, she points to jon, and robin in four-four. listen: plays their parts again; steps against the wood floor, the rhythm, like a chime on the glass of a picture above the piano, a waiter in white; bobbed curls, a black hat; natalia's mother and walker, sharing a bottle of coke—two glasses, a vase of cut flowers where walker and natalia's mother sit, drinking from a straw, a bottle of coke; natalia looks down at her dress; walker, wiping with an apron his hands; we're going out—dan looks, as natalia walks out the door, a splash of water; or into a stream that cuts into a mountain, like a tear across a dress, fabric fading, cut into skirts held up over weeds, over a hill, anastasia walks, carrying a bucket of sand. where do you want to sit? walker pats his hands against the dirt, and we can make a castle with this—. anastasia dumps sand onto the ground, by a stream in the meadow where flowers grow, then she fills the bucket with water, look—we can pour water over the sand, like this—shape the blocks; a castle, with turrets—walker picks flowers for the castle towers or anastasia puts them in her hat until the sun has almost set, walker, it's time to go home. anastasia holds his hand, we need to get going, down the trail, or your father will be worried about you; a ring on her finger, a diamond weighing heavy as the sound of thunder rumbling through the hills, as walker and anastasia hasten away from the clearing, he begins to cry, at the sound of thunder that echoes against the cliffs rising up, feet hitting a trail, walker? anastasia picks him up to carry him, in her arms as she sings out a tune, a melancholy accompaniment to cover the sound of thunder as they cross over the stream, as they wind through the weeds, anastasia carrying walker in her arms until he falls asleep; walker—

across the sky a plane nearing the runway, a roaring that comes like the rough whisper of paper between strings, walker as he dries his eyes; it seems like a long time—is it too early to go fishing yet? no—it isn't even may—in a white t-shirt and black pants, natalia with nadine, across the street, down the walk under the neon lights glowing, close the shutter, the lights are too bright; don't clap your hands, natalia puts her hands together as though to pray, i don't think i could listen to that. what? rain, coming down, cold through the green leaves of trees standing high overhead; smell of pine trees where anastasia sits, unbuttoning her dress, taking off her clothes for a swim; weight of a gold ring, or a chain, bound to split at the seams, the dresses anastasia makes to wear, teaching at the board-ing school; sand castles beside a stream, your great-grandmother, walker says—

what? what did he say—he minds that you're going away? i can't think about that. what happened to engineering, nadine? as walker sits, arms folded across his chest, gazing into a night sky or staring into a stream, they will still be able to make a living, natalia's mother says—do you think she thinks we'll get married? i don't know. why isn't she worried about us? walker is. i think she is; it just doesn't show as much—; under the roof, sound of rain into a tin, feet hitting the trail, natalia says, it makes a nice sound—. can you play this piece? spreads the manuscript over music stands, one part in three-four, another in five-eight— are you going out again—another performance tonight—bow against the body of the violin, a voice that surrounds us, beyond the sounds of a woman humming, singing to herself, a melody, a clear and uncomplicated tune on violin; i wonder where i can get someone to sing this part—. robin asks, do you have the right clothes to wear? we need formal attire; natalia looks at anastasia's picture on the piano, a hat with ribbon, and dresses with lace and bows. dan, picking the picture up, i think she looks like you—but her hair was more auburn, walker says, and long—did she wear it coiled on top of her head, lifting skirts over weeds in the meadow as she walked, as natalia walks to her chamber rehearsal, a beethoven quartet, robin says, mendelssohn violin concerto, playing with an orchestra—

a woman who sings, natalia asks robin, do you know someone with a good voice—you would have to pay her, i think. could you do it, then? bow against strings, listen—some of the rhythms are strange, and unclear—but i hear it in my head, a beautiful uncomplicated melody, one voice above the violin, a melody, notes clear and hollow and long that hover in the air, natalia points, like that bird on the window sill—that's a pigeon, robin says, that made a nest on our roof—we shoot at it with rubber bands, to make it go away. so my notes aren't that clear? if you want it precise, with rhythms like that—i can't read your handwriting, natalia, if you could find a teacher here—i didn't think you wanted to go to school, dan says. no—. a teacher instructing him as he stands at the bar, an arm over his head; lines of dancers across the floor, as dan practices in their apartment, it's too hot in here—can you turn the fan around—i can't concentrate—i don't have to practice now—nadine? what is she doing now, is that a letter from her? i don't know, natalia says; then, she's getting ready to leave. she's going to move, and get a job in another place—what do your parents think? i thought nadine was the one who would do something practical—at least i can perform, and teach, or choreograph; and you can play in chamber groups, or for an orchestra—who's she going out with now? i thought that was interesting about her, how she was always going out with someone new. only because she wasn't interested in anyone, really—what do you mean? rain falling against glass like tears streaking a face, walker? is that you? what did he say, dan asks, does he want to know when you'll come back? no—. then, they aren't as angry at you for leaving before you finished school—they must be worried—yes—finished practicing? a line across the floor, piano phrasing an accompaniment, turns in front of the mirror; hands around her waist like a clock that is spinning, dan? doesn't it seem a bit too hot? yes—by the rails as a train rolls past, steps up stairs, not so young, natalia thinks, as she closes her eyes, reading a book as her sight begins to fail, under the light of a lamp and dan falls asleep—stockhausen on a music box, a ballerina who turns, in a dream, across a sidewalk, leaves blowing with the wind in the trees, brushing leaves like hair—

anastasia puts her diary down. a thousand birds singing in the meadow as anastasia lies on her rock, i wonder what walker is doing now—turns around to see, walker, in a pair of blue overalls, making a house, sticks and weeds; a castle that will crumble to the touch, grass and weeds that blow away across the mountains like the stream where anastasia bathes, pulling pins from her hair, long hair falling down from a ribbon pulled loose, or underneath a straw hat that anastasia wears over her head, as she places her walking stick and takes walker by the hand, down the trail, through the woods, i can smell the fire burning, there—walker points. yes, where your father is sitting, anastasia says; teaching at the boarding school, rows of boys lined up, on desktops, open books like the book that anastasia carries in her hand, pages charred and fraying; walker in the meadow, laying down railroad tracks; anastasia looks up at walker, from the pages of her diary on a desk; marking a page with pen, it is walker starting school; pen across a page, line across a book, on the floor where natalia sits, dan?

so you're going back to school? dan says, i didn't think you would really go back—across the sidewalk like leaves that are blowing, suitcase buckles shut tight; you dance in your company, here i have to teach and perform—even if we're not in the same city, we'll be together still—dan sits down and sighs, head in his hands; i don't even know if i'll get in—. a tie across two notes, a clear, uncomplicated tune, one line, a woman's voice and the violin melody—dan looks, this isn't bad—but it's sloppy, and robin says it's too hard trying to read the notes while you sing; and they don't go, natalia says, exactly with the part on violin—. what about your other pieces? brushes the hair from her eyes, my t-shirt is sticking to my back—natalia gazes out at the street, it doesn't mean that i'm leaving for good; and maybe not at all. will you go home for summer, then? i don't know—or only for a little while—. across the street, listen to that machine—what? that awful clanking noise? it makes an interesting sound; with the sound of that neon light, up there; what a melancholy sound. like the notes of our refrigerator at home—you remember that? because of nadine—is she going away? we'll have to wait and see—

a dress in the making, the fabric that anastasia cuts and sews before lifting the skirt up; pinning cloth, a thousand hooks and eyes; a hat that will catch and blow in the wind, when the angle is right—anastasia puts her notebook down, calls dan? walker turns around, takes off his glasses, natalia should be finding out about school soon—do you think we'll be able to help her go? nadine says, she already supports herself; teaching violin and playing in chamber groups, notes that squawk on small violins, no—it doesn't sound like that—natalia turns a page, what about this one—can you play this one out? eyes brown and wide, focused on her, i didn't practice that this week. you're going to have to practice harder than that; you'll have to study at home, alone, for next week.

you sent him home early? yes—so you could work on your piece. but he hadn't practiced it, anyway. you're going to lose students, if you don't keep them for the whole hour—then, no, i won't, natalia says. they have to practice harder than that, that's all; and why should i spend my time trying to teach, while you get to do what you want all day long—. but dancing is hard work—so is teaching and playing violin—natalia sits down and cries, out of the apartment and the door slams, pictures shake, anastasia's picture that falls off the piano; shatter of glass and dan looks down at the sidewalk, where natalia crosses the street, walking over black pavement and wearing white shoes; underneath a street lamp falls the light mist of rain, a dark night sky and dan stands, hands on his hips, staring at natalia, as she walks away; under a night sky; walker— you're going away? yes—natalia and walker stand underneath the trees; the sound of thunder, an echo before the rain and the sound falls away—did you play one of your pieces for them? no—

the sound of water falls; on the rails past a city, beyond the meadow and trees, past the city where pavement goes on for miles, buildings rising black against the sky; an array of lights and streets, a train across the rails, disappearing beneath wheels; through a tunnel, across a bridge, natalia, carrying her violin; a taxi horn blaring above the sound of feet on the walk, across a bridge where natalia waits; someone on the street, notes of a saxophone where heath stands, looking for natalia by the tracks of a train, a locomotive, steam; you're robin's friend? yes—

green disappearing into black as natalia and heath sit on orange seats, glow of lights, wheels sparking rails, below, an abyss, the silence long as a river that is winding where walker wades, further out, alone, wearing a fishing cap and vest, carrying two bottles of salmon eggs, and a tin of lures, a box of flies, yellow and red feathers tied into a knot that walker casts into the stream before shading his eyes to see; but he can't look into the muddy river water; nor can he see his face reflected in the stream, the rush of the current as he wades out a bit, a fish on the end of his line as he steps to pull it from the stream, fighting on the end of the line; walker decides not to turn it back; he looks up from the water to see the old people, the woman who turns around to stare; gazing up at them, walker puts down his fishing rod on the bank of a stream, sits down on a rock, puts his head in his hands and thinks of natalia; walker takes from his pocket a handkerchief, wipes the sweat from his eyes, tears or mist—

a step on the trail, natalia's mother with nadine, did you know i was here? we only wanted to go hiking; we didn't know, exactly, where you were—. did you get tired, asks nadine; then, i'll fish, for a while—we don't have enough fish for dinner—just so i don't have to clean them, says nadine; taking off her shoes, she wades into the stream; do you want to wear waders? walker asks. but the water isn't cold—it's muddy, her mother remarks. i'll take a bath, when we get home. soon, maybe, natalia will be back—walker takes off his glasses to rub his eyes, then cleans them against the flannel of his shirt; nadine has a fish—walker steps away from the bank, do you want me to help reel it in? no—then, we'll have two fish for tonight—

natalia wipes off the countertops, brushes the crumbs into the trash—i have a better chance in another city, where there isn't so much competition—you're sure you want to go? no—teaching and playing weddings, or for an orchestra, that's what you'll do when you get out of school. but at least i'll have time to compose music, if i'm in school; pull down the blind, the lights are glaring—; neon across the street, pink and purple, an array of white, the flowers anastasia gathers, that she sets in a vase, holding walker's hand; someone who stays away, in the mist; wearing a ribbon in her hair, pink ribbons that flow down her back like the dresses anastasia wears, in the meadow; at the sight of a woman slowly fading, holding the hand of a boy, sitting still at a desk in school, a pen in hand, or carrying a walking stick, jumping over a stream, it is walker, building a sand castle under the sun in the meadow where anastasia sits reading a letter; across the meadow, a small town, growing into a city where anastasia teaches in boarding school; anastasia looks down at her ring; walker, starting school; an electrician, putting in wires, lights that glow across a city, neon, pink and blue, like the dresses anastasia makes, a white quilt across a bed, curtains on a window where anastasia watches, through the window where natalia's mother looks out at the rain; across the mountains, leaves dried and blowing, walker writes natalia, nadine will be leaving soon. but she stays at home more now, studying for school; sometimes, she goes hiking in the woods; does she wear a dress and tennis shoes; does she never scrape her knees, against the pointed branches and rocks, tear the fabric; cut and fraying, a thousand fragments into the sky, blowing across the sidewalk, the light tread of steps on the stairs—why'd you tear it up? i didn't even get in. natalia sits down and cries; nadine, unlacing her shoes to pull them off, walker? he's not back yet. and natalia didn't get into school where dan is—natalia's mother says, she should have the time to do what she likes—; when she was young—leaves, scattered and blowing—at least, nadine says, she's decided on something, now. but she needs the time to study—if she had stayed here—but she couldn't do that, you know how much she hated school—and she was so attached to dan. but if she gets into school somewhere else, she may be leaving him— leaving for good? a ribbon that trails into the sky, a boy flying a kite as string slips through his fingertips and it flies higher into the air, away from the ground, away from the park where natalia sits on a bench, watching the boy as the kite blows away—

a conductor waving her baton as the train pulls away; natalia looks at dan fading under the light of a street lamp, obscured by clouds as her vision fogs from the tears in her eyes that she brushes away, a hand across her face as she gazes into the black, smoky iridescence as dan watches her pull away, on a train, in the middle of may, i'm going home—. a conductor striking at the podium with her baton; playing in an orchestra or in her apartment, natalia pulls down the blinds and turns on the light as music fades from a recording, notes like water falling, ondine; a slow part that sounds like a church bell, the sounds of notes on violin, running above the still chord of a piano; in a cloud of lights, tears, running; walker, carrying a picnic basket and two fishing rods, anastasia and walker's father and mother, through the woods, here's where we'll sit— they take worms from a can, put them on hooks; walker's mother sits down in a green and white lawn chair, did you remember to bring the tea? getting up from the chair to take from the icebox a bottle of coke for walker, and for her husband and anastasia a jar of iced tea, as walker sits with his father, casting a line into the lake, look—his father points to trout and minnows swimming between fronds of grass growing by the waterside a little bit away—walker steps up from the director's chair, reaching down into the pond, the trout glimmering beneath the water surface; if i reach into the water, do you think i could catch one? fish that are slimy and cold, but smooth to his touch—walker wades out a bit, points to a fish, bigger than the rest—but when walker steps out, he makes a splashing sound, scaring the fish away.

in the silence of this mountain meadow, it is walker now who stands, somewhere in the trees, wearing a hat and fishing vest; or is it a woman whose dress is blowing lightly in the current of a breeze, above the sad song of a bird that is singing; natalia, carrying a hat or a fishing creel, a violin; notes that sound clear above the running of a stream on an evening when no moonlight shines down, above a street; can you play this part? heath looks at the notes spread across the page, it isn't easy to read your writing, but the notes are

decipherable, i guess—. i can tell how it sounds, just looking at it—
melody of the bass line, two lines, an octave and a half apart; two
girls who stare at each other in the mirror of a room where natalia
combs her hair; walker says you weren't going out so much—. not
as much, but it's summer now, and i don't feel like staying home. so
you can practice as much as you want, while i'm gone—. but not
while you're here? when you were gone, walker says he got tired
of going fishing alone—standing in a mountain meadow, a man
who looks away into the trees; but i think he is listening, natalia—;
walker says, you liked playing on your own to begin with, even
when you were small, i used to listen to you playing, and i couldn't
understand how you could sit there so long—just waiting—

like a man casting his line above a stream, bubble floating above
the river current; does he see the shadow of a woman fading, where
a boy and a woman are walking away, the woman holding his hand;
a picture of your great-grandmother, walker says, a photograph,
edges fading like the sound of notes on an old phonograph that
jumps and skips, scratches at the edge, near the end of the piece
that natalia plays, don't clap, she prays as she looks at the eyes focused on her; someone who stands in the audience; a row of people
turning to walk away under the bright lights of an auditorium and
natalia wonders, do their shoes sink slightly into the carpet as they
stand and turn to look at her; a face in the glass; why don't you
ever cut your hair? it looks good, i think; anastasia's mother pulls
her hair into three parts, but i think we should make a braid—rebecca sighs, i thought my children were going to have a spinster
aunt. anastasia shrugs, it might have been better that way—but
you're in love with him—. i could have just kept working, teaching in the boarding school. and end up all alone? a gown rustling
over a silk slip, we should pick flowers, and put them in a vase; at
the sight of smoke from a locomotive rumbling, steam; a suitcase
shut tight; a dress or a bouquet of flowers she is holding, anastasia
with her mother and father now, a week in the city—then back to
the boarding school; a white dress with silk flowers that anastasia makes, it's too tight, her mother says, it's about to burst at the
seams. no, it won't. don't braid my hair—. you always looked nice,

anastasia, with your hair pulled back; a thousand hooks and eyes, anastasia looks in the mirror, look at the yards of fabric, dear reader, can you see this woman dressed in white? does her long hair flow in waves smooth as this river current; does a tear flow down her face—gaze into the glass, you will see another woman; a man who stands in the meadow alone, shutting both his eyes; does he fall into the grass, a pool of flowers at his feet, while anastasia and her mother sit, staring into an abyss, a black night falling; beneath the moon that clouds a face as they tear the dirt away, digging into the grass, green disappearing into black, soft dirt falling over wood, or sand, ashes dried and blowing across the meadow, a woman taking a boy's hand; with the clear sound of a woman singing comes the sound of a violin; she holds her mother in her arms; an abyss; a wedding ring on her hand glowing gold in the sun, under the full moon that rises above where walker and natalia sit, we were worried about you, leaving by yourself—but i was living with dan.

across the sky, a plane flying, over the hills while walker sits drying his eyes—you're home—for a little while—can we put these in a vase? on the table where natalia and her mother sit; across the mountains and trees, god might be waiting for someone, or staring into the mist, at the sound of two notes fading; a woman standing, silent and still, on a hillside, wearing an apron, flowers filling her hands as she turns to look at an audience; a bouquet thrown over a banister, or onto a stage, petals that scatter across the white tiles, petals; natalia, holding a violin and she steps, the black behind the curtain, eyes focusing like starlight, on a photograph of anastasia, sitting still on the piano as natalia works, writing notes—what was that sound? what did she say? that one day, a woman in a pink gown will walk down a hillside carrying flowers, or a girl—one day, the solid image of a man will fade into the mist; silence that descends over a rooftop where natalia sleeps with dan, the sound of thunder, the night sky like sleep covering an abysmal noise, cacophony of strings as natalia walks down the hall, looking for a practice room, in here? she puts her notebooks down, turns on the light—it's too small—not like the churches where i used to play, isn't there a church around here? but i wouldn't go there alone; not by myself, heath says. but i always played in churches alone—

across the cities, wisps of smoke wafting, a yellow glow of lights like stars that light the way across the sky, a plane roaring in the distance; nadine, sitting, still, and reading a book; above the tiles, hands of a white clock spinning; voice of a thousand angels raised to the pitch of a plane engine, through the clouds, wisp of smoke in the air; the sound of voices fading, turns across the floor; i'm going, i guess—; natalia says, it's not the best school, but at least i got a scholarship—i'll make enough money, if i teach or play in a chamber group; she looks at dan, i can always drop out. she sits down in a chair, out of breath; standing by the window, gazing out at the people below, dan says, we won't be together, then—i didn't know you'd think about it like that—i won't be far away. but you won't be living here—think about that: a woman standing in a field, holding a hat; under a cloudy sky, when no sun shines through, the heat in a mountain meadow, sweltering under a sun that can't be seen, anastasia turns through the field and is gone; i thought you weren't worried about that; natalia walks across the floor, i'm going to call walker—; across the wires, a phone that is ringing; an image that turns to dust, natalia thinks of the buildings that stand as she walks away, fading, a fray in the fabric, do the lights of the city dim; pieces of fabric cut and fraying as she and dan sit, red velvet seats; a city that fades under a plane into a blur of lights; i'm coming home in may—

her mother puts dishes on the table; sound of music floating, in the heat of a spring day, the windows open, natalia says, i like the noise; machines, a sound above the violin, a flute and piano, an oboe, a clarinet, a woman who comes down a trail holding a hat, turns in the wind, a trill on the piano that sounds like the whistle of a bird; i'm leaving, i think—does he begin to cry, tears that form a puddle at his feet, over the ribbons on a pair of dancing shoes, like eyes hidden from view by the mist, the trees; a vase holding cut flowers, natalia, taking walker's hand, i'm back, for the summer—an apartment emptied of pictures; harp strings and women robed in white, the sound of thunder, rain; natalia says to nadine,

what did he say? tell him, i won't be far away; a track snaking between cities, black rails covering green; a tunnel, disappearing into
black, the notes natalia writes, a part for percussion instruments;
heath says, maybe you better spend some time on violin—natalia
shrugs, i know those pieces well enough, i spent three hours today,
and two hours in class—. listening to recordings, in the confines
of a room, rain falling; drops streaking the glass of a windowpane
as walker drives away, and now nadine, he looks at their mother, is
gone—; across the cities, across the ocean, mountains and trees, in
the clear light of a woman singing beneath a spotlight as though
underneath the moon where natalia and walker walk further up
a trail, through pine trees, drops of water from branches falling
down; a stream winding down a mountaintop like a highway down
a hillside, streets, the lights glowing, there was no place to go, no-
where to get away—; don't you want to go back, nadine asks, to play
music there—

the red hand of a streetlight flashing, cross with the lights, it's
faster, heath says, look—the green and white awning of a cafe,
notes across the lines, in her sleep or in a classroom at school, writing notes as her teacher lectures in a white room at school, listen—
natalia tries to write out the rhythms she hears in class, no—her
teacher says, it doesn't sound like that—as long as it sounds interesting—heath plays the rhythms; the light across the street, look—
how do you do that, natalia asks. in the rhythm of an orange hand
flashing, stop—heath pulls her back, listen—the rhythm, and then
you add more notes, here—blare of a taxi horn, a saxophone, on
the street, notes carried on a subway train, natalia writes walker on
staff paper, green disappearing into black, a ribbon bound around a
hat, woven like braids, hair falling down, notes that sound like rain
through the trees or ocean waves crashing against a shore, a harbor, where boats come in, from across the sea, ocean waves carrying
grains of sand that arrive on a beach, in the shell of an oyster, a pearl
that anastasia finds; pulling her hair up, pinning it beneath her hat,
standing on a beach where walker runs, drawing his toes through
the sand, under the sun that shines brightly over the waves, anastasia shades her eyes against the setting sun, ribbons of color, layers of

lavender and orange, under the clouds full as the dress that anastasia lifts over rocks to walk; walker, wearing overalls; it doesn't look as good on you—don't, her teacher says, wear a tuxedo—but i can't move in a dress—you better tie your hair up , or it will get in your way—heath pulls her hair back; natalia, turning on lights in the bare room of an apartment, white walls and wood floors, a hallway, a door—this is where you practice? a black grand piano, heath runs his fingers across the instrument; anastasia, running with walker through the grass, her hat in hand until she falls, a meadow of flowers that is growing, where do they go, natalia? nadine looks up at the stars; walker, tearing through the weeds, building a sand castle; anastasia's husband laying down wires, across a hillside, lights that glow from a window; waiting, someone who holds a fishing rod in hand, a creel full of trout from a stream, a bouquet of flowers picked in a meadow, set in a vase; across the ocean, a wave, a boat across the sea; walker's eyes as he turns to look: a thousand eyes on the orchestra, natalia as she ties heath's bow tie and he combs his hair back before walking to his chair, i'll be waiting for you—

a hand signaling to stop, an arm around a waist, steps across black pavement, an awning, an abyss; canyon walls plummeting to the earth, drops of rain that fall from clouds that form above the mountain, by a clear running stream where no one stands, now; under a plane across the sky, a memory that looks better in the past, when distance has aged reality, put a perspective on a time covered with dreams; can you see the future now, its complications and twists; will walker appear to pick flowers in the field; will he grasp at certain truth only to come up for air, holding a grain of sand in his palm, will it vanish with the current that carries it, to a pool of water, to a young girl walking down a trail and holding a flower in her hand, or wearing a ring, hair wrapped in coils around her head like the snake that lies on a rock then slithers slowly into the trees, into the dark; open your eyes—carry me across, i'm getting tired— a voice that sings in the dark of a room, dark skin and hair pulled back, natalia looks through a small window in the doorway of the practice room; she thinks of churches with glass windows brightly stained, a cathedral, the halls dark and long, red carpet beneath feet, on stage an echo, words carried across a congregation, repetition of notes like ocean waves crashing, on violin strings, changing harmonies from a major to minor key, span of gull wings stretching, birds that make a discordant sound as a boat comes into harbor, the woman in the practice room, does she pray, in a forest, collecting sun rays like leaves, reflected off the water, gold band around her neck, a woman dressed in black, standing on stage as she sings, is it only a percussive echoing across the wires of a ringing telephone, in the meadow, in the past, ashes that scatter or sit on a window sill in a vase; charred and fraying, a past; or put together like cut glass on a table, a pencil and glue, a notebook—what does she say? that one day, a woman's life will fade like the sound of a distant horn, gold and brass, the instruments that play a part; a woman dressed in black with a gold band around her neck as she turns; in a field, a woman who appears bearing alms, or cutting with a scythe in a circular motion a ream of wheat in the fields beneath an airplane, patches like a quilt in green and brown, fields that go on for miles—

natalia shuts her eyes, a triangle, quarter tones, a restless sigh, across the room, heath puts his pencil down, on his desk, a restless sound, pounding of feet down a corridor as the clock chimes, through the walls, sounds that rise up and echo, a woman playing harp in a robe with sleeves that billow in the wind, gleaming under the lights of a stage, the light reflected from the brass instruments and the shine on the piano, a woman who stands next to the piano; beyond the clouds above, in the sky, nadine, reading a book; filling out forms or writing at a desk, across a wood floor where dan sits, drying his eyes, sound of wind blowing through a crack in the window as he stretches his legs on the window sill, looking out beyond the glass, an array of lights and streets below, people on a sidewalk wandering as though on a trail, the fan that blows in the room where natalia sleeps alone; on a plane in a night sky, nadine writes a letter; a job in a bookstore; and natalia thinks, i still don't have enough time—lying awake at night or looking out the window, staring at the stars above her; playing in an orchestra—ondine, sound of a church bell striking, a clock at school; reading the backs of record jackets, look, heath, mendelssohn when he was seventeen—as she

puts together the pages of all the notes she has written down; erika
in the room next to her, singing out notes, a part for violin and percussion instruments, quick heels across white tiles, a woman carrying a hat who sings above a symphony, natalia asks, erika, can you
read this part? notes slow and held long as natalia writes a piano
accompaniment; she writes a letter to nadine, arriving in a city, on
a bus, fields that flow by her, the hills green and rolling, that carry
her past her childhood, a math book on a desk, rocks beneath her
feet, a field, across the wires, electricity—

under the street lamps, misty glow in the rain and there you
stand, gazing up at the moon, clear and dark, the water, the trees;
a chest of clothes thrown open at a hotel where anastasia unpacks,
smoothing wrinkles out of a dress and hanging it up, on its perch in
a cage a parrot that sings, dust colored bedspreads, and by the bed a
writing desk, a vase holding cut flowers, a lamp without a shade; nadine looks out the window; two girls staring into a mirror until the
old woman gets up from her chair and looks toward walker; a man
and a woman, drinking a bottle of coke from a straw, shared demise;
a dress cut, in the making, or being pulled apart by the seams, between the lines; nadine, on the balcony of an apartment building,
listening to music; a harbor with boats, flagstone steps across a park;
a militiaman on a horse, what is he looking for, natalia? behind the
face, behind the mask, impenetrable as the moon—

walker takes off his hat, in the beginning of autumn, standing
alone, casting his line into a stream; does he shade his eyes to look
into the distance, as he thinks about the past: a girl who once stood
in waders, singing softly to herself; or a girl who sits by a fireside
wearing a dress, poking the frying fish with a long pointed stick;
a man wearing a uniform who lifts his hand in salute, a man who
walks past him, still further up the trail, holding a fishing rod and
carrying a creel in his hand, does he wear a hat, does he stare into
the trees, as they begin to groan, under the weight of a breeze, a
sigh that is stirring, someone turning under the light, a woman
who picks her instrument up, a woman with a gold band around
her neck in a black dress as she sings, under the glaring lights as an
audience sits in red velvet seats; gazing at the gold, the brass of an

instrument, a note that is played at the wave of a baton, wearing black pants and a white shirt, tying a bow tie, as the performance is about to begin, natalia feels like covering her eyes, turning to walk up the aisle, feeling like the carpet that sinks slightly beneath her feet, smoke that rises like ocean waves against a shore; falling into the black of the abyss, she thinks, i could disappear for good, green into black; at the strike of her baton, a flute begins to play above a piano accompaniment, as the violins begin to play like rain against a windowpane or tears against a face, holding the last note until the sound disappears; a bouquet of flowers thrown on stage, one disappears into the abyss, under the bright lights shining and natalia imagines walking on a trail as she walks behind the red velvet curtains, steps echoing against the walls that rise up like the canyon; natalia, wake up—

heath looks down at her, eyes focused on her like pinpoints of stars, eyes below her, on stage in front of an audience, in the field, does walker pick her up to carry her in his arms, under the sun that has almost set, into an abyss, ashes, a fire; trails of smoke disappearing into a black sky; an audience silent as the stars as natalia turns behind the curtain of a stage, a woman, or a girl wearing waders and three copper bracelets on her arm; descending into the silence, in the black, a waiter who brings two bottles of coke, wearing a white apron and black tie where walker and celia sit now, in a cafe; it's nine, heath says; don't you think you shouldn't miss class—natalia says, but i can't do everything at the same time; turns a sheet of paper in class, hears a rustle and wonders, what was that sound—as she stands by a train track and feels a restlessness as she shuts her eyes to see, the image of tracks and a train that stands in front of her now, turning into the sound of a stream; notes that flow past her, drops of water into a stream, where do they go, natalia? into the ocean; heath, calling natalia from the sidewalk, you better wake up—

a woman who gazes at the street running beside her, shiny cars wet under the rain and a puddle beneath her feet, a white walk turning to grey from the water coming down or fog rolling over the buildings that obscure her view, so that she cannot see walker now, cannot think nor imagine what natalia might be doing under the sunlight that comes through her window as she lies in bed and heath calls from the sidewalk, not letting her rest; you're going to be late for class—heath walks away as natalia sits up in bed and throws on a robe to follow him, down the stairs, out the door; but heath is already gone, down the sidewalk where leaves blow in the wind—

natalia thinks, as she starts to get dressed, was it only a dream, notes that come in her sleep, as she walks down the street, clack of an orange train across tracks and natalia walks beneath the bridge carrying her bag; heath opens the building door as the clock reads nine o'clock, and natalia hurries to catch up to him; as she opens the door and walks inside, she thinks of nadine, writing a letter to her; you better hurry up, natalia writes, you better figure out what you want to do—but i have plenty of time—natalia sits at her desk watching the clock and heath on the far side of the room; she takes her notebook out as her teacher plays out the notes and natalia writes them down; but the rhythms aren't exactly right, her teacher says, even if you know all the notes. i missed one note, heath says; but all my rhythms are right. because you play drums. are you going to practice, or go to class? as they are walking down the hall, i guess i better go to class—maybe, natalia says, i could just study composition—but you haven't written enough yet. how many pages do you need? more than you've got. how're you do-ing in counterpoint? and natalia thinks, george crumb, paper clips on piano strings; heath asks, don't you think it's something you should know, if you're going to write—and natalia can't decide, as she listens to her teacher explain the notes, a prelude, notes in numbers and labeled chords; natalia takes the fugue into a practice room, looks up at the clock, hands around the center, spinning, across the sidewalk, in a dream, waiting; throwing clothes into a bag, i'll take a train, and only miss one day of class, she says to heath, and i'm taking my analysis along, to finish it up on the trip. standing in the doorway, heath asks, do you think he'll have time for you while you're there? he'll have rehearsals, but i'll have money, for once—i can go to a concert, or the museum—

in a park at night, the air still and warm as dan leans against her, over her shoulder, a globe held by a man made out of brass, in the air, white columns of a building beside a garden where a trio plays john cage; i don't know what i think about that—that one day, a man in a meadow will turn to stand alone, gazing into the trees or staring at a stream to see his reflection shake minutely, a fragment, just a little bit; that a woman holding flowers in the folds of an apron will lie on a rock, wearing a ring, and sigh at an array of flowers placed; cast in stone, the lines that natalia follows, wires across the land, light connecting one city to the next; the train that connects two cities by a track once laid down by a boy, who ran with his grandmother through the weeds where she put flowers into a hat, or picked him up to carry him as he began to cry; a boy who wears cotton flannel pants, a suit, as anastasia and her husband travel by car to a different town, staying in a hotel; this is where i will live, walker says, as the car pulls away from the mountains and trees, leaving behind it a trail of dust—this is where i will stay, walker thinks, as he watches the road disappear behind him, underneath the wheels; on a train that is leaving—

i'm trying to understand this counterpoint, natalia says to the man next to her; then, why do you ask? out the window as the land rolls by and she puts her notebook down, closing her eyes—across the sky, under the sun a sound that comes tearing; whether we're together or not—as dan holds her in his arms, even if we have to wait, if it's sometime in the future—down the steps of a church, up an aisle where someone waits in a black robe, or below a cross with arms that enfold her—but what about the time spent just waiting, like in a dream—what do you mean? that one day, the picture of a man and woman will fade, drinking a bottle of coke, shared demise; like dots in the mist, a bridge over a river, gold spanning an abyss; i hadn't thought about that—what about just spending time together—we hardly do that. natalia sits down in the apartment she has left and she thinks, it's already been five months; and we're together, still, natalia says—i don't have time, to see anyone else. heath, in a practice room, notes on violin—or listening to a recording at home, in the dark, erika, as she sings—we're going to perform another piece—something that you wrote—yes—

above a stream running the notes of a violin; a girl looking through the tears that cloud her vision like mist, so that she cannot see her father who has wandered up the trail, wearing green waders and a cream colored fishing vest; standing somewhere in the trees, a woman who gathers flowers, hiking with a girl who wears a dress, who cut her hair short when the length was so long that into the looking glass she would look and see nothing else, under a starry night, dark sky surrounding her, a woman carrying a hat with ribbon, a walking stick; does she shade her eyes to see, into the future, a gold ring like a halo around hair, or stars around the sun; dear reader, where does this sound come from, under a fiery sun, an inconsequential moon that brings together these dancers wearing white shoes, beside a sidewalk cafe; clearing the vision of a woman, rain falling, cold through the veil that cloaks her face, the silence as it descends like mist; is there a point in time beyond the silence where meaning lies, still as a river current; a hatpin, a pearl in the palm of a woman, a reminder of the past, when a ribbon ran through the hand of a girl like a river down a hillside or tears against a face; fallen fragments of moonlight, falling; staring, from the face that sits still in a picture, placed, anastasia, in the meadow when she appears; is there something within the silence, notes in a line across staff paper, green disappearing into black, gold and brass, on the black and white keys of a piano, a sound beyond the flowers growing, before the crash of cymbals like thunder, following the flash of lightning above a stream that strikes and is gone, into the silence where it came from, dear reader, where is that? natalia rubs her eyes, walker? she asks. but it is only dan shaking her, natalia, it's time to get up. i dreamed, she says, of the meadow, going fishing again. in the city where traffic goes by under the street lamps that create a light in the mist; feet; the sound of feet hitting a trail on a dark night when no sun shines through the windows, the light across the street—they closed the theater down—a spotlight that shines down, a woman on stage, singing a song—

beside an ocean, rolling hills and trolley cars, buildings that rise to sway high above the earth; natalia walks to parks and museums while dan is at rehearsal, or she plays on violin; at night, notes carried across the ocean on a wave, notes of a piano, harp strings that sound, in the sculpture garden of the art museum, an arm around her waist; haven't i seen you somewhere before, in the confines of a room or sewing up a dress, gazing out a window, up at the sky, or putting cut flowers on a desk, a photograph on a piano, a part composed on violin; a dance piece, a piece for piano, someone on stage in a black shirt and white tights as natalia practices; crossing the street, a man with blond hair, i think i've seen you—yes—on the train, natalia says, you sat next to me. i work in that building, over there—a lawyer, natalia asks—the light turns and they walk across, down the sidewalk as he waves and heath makes no remark; then, are you interested in him? i don't have time for that. besides, there is no one else, for either of us—a woman in a dress, walking through the fields, alone; a picture on nadine's dresser; my sister, nadine says; she looks so much like you—with long hair; she is older, a little bit—at night, in her sleep, through her dreams a woman walking in a long skirt with black boots, carrying a walking stick—

sometimes did her parents worry, had she gotten lost for good, under a starry night, a full moon above; could voices be heard, calling out her name—natalia? can you hear me, walker asks. heath says, you just fainted—she sits up and wipes her eyes as heath helps her up—it's over—this way, we can walk; it's a better view—across a bridge, span of gold wire across the water, clear and dark; natalia thinks of a mountain stream, where she and walker would go, up a trail—cold and dark, the water—a girl sitting by a brook, waiting for her father to appear on the trail, the sun shining down through the trees, as the pavement disappears, as though from hawkes point to north point, across the distance north and west, to a time that causes natalia to remember, a time not so far gone, in the past; across black pavement, wearing white shoes, into the future now, it is after the fact—

across a bridge, a woman with dark skin who sings; erika, wearing sun glasses as she crosses the street; natalia asks, what is that— i was listening to nina simone—notes slow and held long, i wish i could sing like that—erika says, i sing mostly classical—natalia puts plates on the table, as the clock chimes; erika asks, how much have you written now? a piece for flute, piano, and violin, another for orchestra—a woman wearing a white robe underneath a spotlight, sleeves that billow in the wind—someone who sighs, pulls her hair up, off her neck; black hair hanging down, or tied in a ribbon behind her head, walking up a hill, nadine, in another city, walking through the music conservatory; down the corridors, she looks in practice rooms, stopping to listen as the students practice on their instruments; then, out the door, past houses in rows, white shutters and bright cars, down the hill and on a trolley car that takes her near the ocean, to the bookstore where she works, and she thinks, as she thinks about going back to school, maybe natalia was right—; notes of the piano accompaniment, do you like this part? yes—the pentecostal church, heath asks; you don't have to believe in it, heath—just listen—

a man who sits in an audience and takes off his glasses to wipe his eyes, a handkerchief in his hand; sitting in a cafe, across from natalia in a red shirt and black pants, eyes like dark pools that form by a clear and running stream where she stood gazing at her reflection as it shook minutely, a fragment—; someone puts the book he is reading down, as natalia gets up from her table, does he see the sight of a woman fading, carrying a violin or a stack of music books, staff paper, behind the curtain, on stage, natalia conducting the orchestra as erika sings, in a gold dress with black shoes, underneath a street lamp falls the light mist of rain, gold glowing against black, underneath the awning, a performance, cameo, green and white; from within the silence the sound of two maracas shaking, light shining on a woman singing on stage, petals, flowers, the sound of applause that is fading before natalia turns to walk away, holding a bouquet of flowers, click of heels across white tiles, down the street where neon lights are reflected beneath her feet, the puddles and they step, as it rains, i didn't know it would sound like that—

that one day, a woman in a red dress would be singing over the sound of someone humming, singing from a long way off, creating a melancholy sound; is it someone in the background, singing a mournful tune from the chorus of violins that begin to play, chairs in rows across a green lawn, the silence that lifts as though a veil;

clear and dark, someone singing from a long way off, as clear and precise as a woman sitting alone and wearing a hat, as walker runs through the woods, collecting notes like leaves, under a dark sky as the thunder claps; can you see, through the silence, someone singing as though in a church, in the wings, on the stairs, down an aisle, creating a cacophony of dissident voices, carried over the waves, smooth as a sailing ship, not so distraught, now, as the past disappears behind, underneath these wheels, the sound of a fog-horn fading, a trumpet note that hovers and then dies in the air, gold or brass; carry me across—two notes carried as though across a distant stream where someone stands fishing; casting a line into a stream, it is walker, i'm getting behind; it is the woman who turns around, wearing dark glasses and sitting in the director's chair, holding a fishing rod before she decides to stand, a dress tearing at the seams, forking, a road, as walker looks beyond the dust stirred by the wheels, hovering in the air; not so young, at this time; a thought fading, a clock that turns, hands around the center, shatter of glass, rain of dust beyond a windowpane, circling the clear light of the moon, a woman's voice that sounds and then fades, beyond the glass, into the silence that begins to stir ashes above a fire, trans-lucent echo shrill as whistling in the dark, in the wake of a blurred image, from across the bridge, steps and there you stand, clear and dark the water, the running of a stream, in the rain, eyes that look out beyond the glass, beyond the reflection of a girl spinning, a leaf, a page of music that falls to the floor and blows across the sidewalk, carried by the wind like leaves, that scatter under the drops of rain that fall slowly from the sky; a man who is writing, wearing dark glasses to shield his eyes from the sun; does he look into the dis-tance, into the clearing where a woman wearing a long dress listens to a boy; does she carry him in her arms—

across the meadow, the sound of a train whistle wailing, a loco-motive, steam; a car that gathers speed over a dirt road that snakes through the woods, like a stream; dust that hovers in the air and then falls, disappearing, underneath a cloudburst, rain, a puddle where a young girl sits, as her father walks away, looking up at the trees; hair, fallen fragments of moonlight falling, flowing like the reflection of stars in a stream, the face of a woman who looks, follow her gaze beyond the place where silence falls, smooth as the surface of a pond, in the palms of a woman, water that she puts to her lips to drink, to connect the notes that create a dissonant sound, lines changed to notes played on brass or string, wrapped around a peg that natalia turns, bow across a string creating a sound, crossed by harmonies, a bridge, a span of wire, paper clips on strings or pencils that create a rasping sound; the letters that walker writes to his father, in a uniform, across the wires; on a radio, songs played by a woman who first wrote the notes down, alone; calling from a long way off, the voice of a woman who asks a question that won't be answered yet, contortions of a wave that turns into sound, like a ribbon bound to a hat, a corset, constricting squeeze of a boa constrictor, in a garret, until it is free, tumbling from a tower, like a lock of hair through the air, falling to the ground, tumbling and then a girl stands, in the dark to pray, looking up at the pulpit or out to the moon, where a voice connects to the tides washing this image up on the beach, a woman in a long flowing gown who sits up and cries, taking a handkerchief from a man's hand, wearing cotton flannel pants, a suit and hat, peach ribbon turned around the brim, a black feather, yellow and red that he sets on his head, turning to walk away as a woman holds the handkerchief in her hand, in a ball, constricting it in her hand before she shakes it out to wave, at a man who walks away, holding a cane, a hat, a tall man striding into the distance, a ring on his finger, a gold band; a man who wears glasses, gold around the rim, black hair blowing in the breeze as he wears waders, casting a line into the stream, lifting the fly before dropping it again; over the rocks he walks, as a boy over a beach holding the hand of a woman whose hair is graying, her daughter, across the fields, does she shade her eyes against the sun before putting on dark glasses, running through the weeds, carrying a message from afar to a man, is it walker, or a woman writing notes steadily with a pen, black letters across a page taken from a notebook, locked up in the confines of a desk drawer, found beside a dresser, a bed with rose colored bedspreads, a lamp, under the light that is glowing, two girls whose eyes cover the surface of a page, a message carried as though in a bottle, that anastasia has written, black feather pen across a page, like a car across a road or a trail where a woman walks, lifting her skirts over weeds, growing older as she stands and shades her eyes to see, america—where has she gone—i don't know, her husband says, light a candle in the window for her—

across the meadow, as though in a dream, america grows beneath the confines of her mother's skirt, underneath anastasia's hand—a girl who will grow into a woman, at the turning of a page, the clapping of hands that hold a hat, pulled by the current of a breeze, satin ribbon trailing as anastasia makes garlands in the sun, and someone waits, looking for america to be born before the message has arrived, a girl who will dress herself in crimson, bob her black hair and wear black hats, write a letter to a man, will you marry me or carry my child; does it make a difference now, dear reader, or no matter how you look at the lines, does this story only go one way, across a certain path that is turning in the fields, through the woods, trees that grow tall and green, merging into black, above timberline, where natalia's mother stands on top of a peak, snow covering rocks that scatter and fall into a pond, creating a ripple below, it is walker who sees the reflection of the old man and woman, sitting in green and white lawn chairs as they cast their lines into a stream, waiting, for the strike of a fish swimming in the pool below, underneath the water, surfacing; the gentle drumming of rain on the surface of a window glass, in streaks that run in lines like tears down a face, clearing the vision of a woman, the constant sound of water running, as constant as a gaze, at the sound of someone calling from a distance, a voice that rises like steam or smoke, carried like a message from far away, under the confines of a skirt of a woman who is singing a melancholy tune, holding her hand to the heart of a girl who is waiting to be born; her voice when it is heard, a cry of notes, does someone pick her up and carry her, into her mother's arms; does someone say, a girl who will one day wear a crimson dress with white lace, a black hat as she looks, is she lost, a woman who cut her hair, black curls beneath a dark velvet hat, mittens to keep her hands warm, until she writes a letter to someone across the miles, carried through the rain, the voice of a girl; into the black, smoky iridescence as a plane pulls away and natalia closes her eyes to sleep, as the plane carries her beyond the mountains and trees, like a woman who carries a girl across time, from the dark confines beneath her skirt to the light of day, a scream at the light streaming yellow through a windowpane, a girl in a white cap tied with a ribbon on her head, a pale blue ribbon and white pants with ribbons at the knees, blue eyes open wide, she looks at anastasia as she looks out a window or leans against a tree, walking up a trail with a walking stick and holding a girl who sings quietly to herself as her mother carries her up the trail and sets her down in the sun, a meadow of flowers where america plays, patting the dirt with her hands, feeling the mud squish beneath her toes as she walks by the side of a stream, holding anastasia's hand; does she carry a walking stick to stir the mud, write a message in the sand, the letters that anastasia tries to decipher as she walks by the stream as a girl, lifting her skirts and holding a hat and walking stick in hand, pink ribbon tied around the rim, like the ribbon on a pair of dancing shoes, spins and turns, and she is gone, like smoke or steam that disappears through the air; or a conversation whispered between two girls, one who shakes out her hair to let it flow in the breeze behind her, at a distance, in her past, the clear sound of a robin calling from above her in the trees; a question formed on the lips of a singer like a kiss that wafts into the air, floating before spinning down, as though leaves carried by an ocean current, or lightning that strikes down a tree where a girl once sat, reading a book; charred and fraying, across the lines, a girl who spins out stories like strings of beads worn by her grandmother, in a picture that natalia keeps on top of a piano, above the keys that she strikes, writing a melody—

the voice of a woman singing, as natalia listens, does someone lift her up to carry her, across the field where no woman has been seen; a man silent and still, can you see him on the mountainside, walking by himself, down a hill where no trees grow, above the timberline, toward a clear and running brook, a pond, the old woman and the man as they get up and fold their director's chairs, moving them to another spot, a few feet away; as the woman opens the ice chest and looks inside, walker thinks, does he have something to say; something to tell them now, walking down a hill, wearing a hat and fishing vest, two fish in his creel that he will clean when he gets to the pond; the water, cold and clear; rocks lining the bottom of the pond, nothing growing here, as he waves at the woman who lowers dark glasses from her eyes; walker sets down his fishing equipment and takes the fish from his creel; he cleans them before taking off his glasses, dipping them into the pond, wiping the water away from the lenses until they are clean; he puts them back over his eyes and stares at the clearing that surrounds him; purple and yellow flowers that grow in the meadow, grass that waves in the wind and grows by a rock where a young woman sits, brushing her hair before tying it up and tucking it under her hat, lacing her black boots, lifting skirts over weeds, a full skirt and pink, that flares up and then falls back down, like her hair, floating in loose strands; or the flowers that she holds, that she has picked for her mother, will they put these in a vase.

walker watches as she shades her eyes against the sun setting over the mountain, walker and his daughter, the people in the director's chairs; what do they patiently await, dear reader, as walker walks down the trail holding his fishing rod, wearing a vest and creel, or holding the hand of a girl who looks at a woman in a pink gown, who stands to shake out her hair, takes out the pins, soaps and washes it in the cold of the pond, runs her toes through the water, sand or grass, creating letters with her hand; when natalia leaves the mountain meadow, when she lets go of walker's hand, from her eyes the tears that begin to fall, down her face, in a stream, drops of water carried by the river current, into a pool where anastasia bathes and finds a pearl, a hatpin; a doll clothed in a long dress that nadine carries with her before the moment stands still against a soft whispering, hands around a clock creating a barely audible whir, words written from the pen of a man who speaks, a boy, a girl who steps in and seems as though from a dream wafting over a mountaintop, above a river, carrying notes from a river current; i am not one to speak so slowly, natalia thinks, as america forms her first words; speaking as though in slow motion, hands moving in gestures, signs, until there is a clear sound of someone singing, an unexpected tune, carried beyond the fields to another place, not so fraught with memory, even as the strings of an instrument resonate with the emotions of a girl who conducts an orchestra; a man whose eyes are focused on her, clear and dark, haven't i seen you before—

creating an accompaniment to the voices that sing under the rain, under the street lamps, misty glow and there you stand, clear as a river current, a breeze waiting to be felt, next to skin like silk, the rustle of a dress, a woman who holds a bouquet of flowers beneath a balcony, wearing silk, in a tuxedo, black and white, the red of a rose that she holds in her hand, a chorus of women's voices, harp strings, violin; the sad song when a woman appears in the meadow, what does this mean, the sound of notes, running, a girl in a crimson dress with white lace gathering flowers; a look into the past or into a mirror at a woman wearing full skirts, a wedding band on her finger like the gold around the neck of a woman as she sings in a black dress, the melody of a girl born at a time that remains to be seen; walking down the sidewalk in black pants, wearing white shoes, up steps, an open door, someone who disappears into the silence and then returns, piano notes heard beneath a window or flowing out from beneath a door, beneath black and white photographs, a girl who sits beside anastasia, planning lessons for school; does anastasia carry her in her arms, when america cries out, breaking the silence that hovers around them like mist, in a frame house, a small town, an electrician laying down wires, across the cities, streets—

nadine, on the sidewalk, black pavement sloping steeply to the ocean, trolley cars beside waves that rise and recede; heath picks up his violin, strings across wood like a bridge, playing a melody as natalia plays on piano and erika sings; a composer whose sight is fading, in the dark night of a room; someone steps into the black beyond the moon, raising arms to the sky, in a forest, stepping down a trail, leaves that crunch beneath feet like shells; leaving a past behind, walking on a beach away from the waves, toward a white wood frame house, a bed of roses, a house with shutters, black trim; anastasia pulls down the window blinds, smoothes the quilt on the bed, smoothing wrinkles from her skirt, does she wear a white gown with white lace and silk flowers, a dress made in the confines of a room; a train, as she walks, a bouquet of red roses, a ring; eyes focused on the podium, a man in a black gown who begins to speak; down the aisles, between church pews, red carpet that sinks beneath her feet, does someone pick her up to carry her across the meadow, smooth as a sailing ship, to a time not so fraught with memories, even as the past slips behind, slowly, as anastasia steps beside an ocean, walking on a beach, carrying america beneath her skirts that billow in the wind, a child that grows beneath the hand of a woman wearing a ring; a current that ebbs and flows on the sand of this beach, a hatpin, a pearl; a girl that anastasia gives birth to in the confines of a room, where a man waits for the message of a girl; waiting to be born, into the hands of a man who gives her to anastasia, a man who comes through the door, lifts her and carries her, a tear that falls, into the abyss; a girl who looks from the place where she rests with anastasia, eyes closed, singing a melody as anastasia thinks to name her; america—

on a beach, patting the dirt with her hands, in a dark room until anastasia's husband opens the blinds, letting in beams of sunlight that angle against the wood floor that robert walks across, as across the miles anastasia looks, into the eyes of a girl, blue eyes open wide under a canopy, beside a bureau where a picture of anastasia sits, in a long dress with white lace; a hat, pink or blue ribbon bound around the rim; a walking stick in hand as she walks across the fields, a dirt trail, shading her eyes against the sun that shines brightly on the people below, fishing from the director's chairs, casting their lines into a pond, the woman with dark glasses looks at anastasia now, wind rippling through her hair, rustle of skirts in the wind as she listens to the call of a whippoorwill; what is this strange and sudden sound, a bird singing above the running water where anastasia bathes her feet, running her toes through the sand, marking letters with her walking stick that the old woman reads, taking off her glasses to decipher the meaning, on a day when the sun shines through the clear blue to trees below, that grow tall on the hillside; the sound of a stream, the sigh of a woman, stars with pinpoint focus on anastasia, smooth satin ribbon of a hat, silk flowers on the pink dress of a doll that nadine carries, walking with her mother, hiking steeply up a hill to the place where anastasia looks, over a hillside covered with city lights, blue and pink like stars, or the lights of a runway lighting the way home, two candles in a window; someone looking for a girl wearing a crimson dress with white trim, walking alone, through the mountains, sleeping underneath a tree, starlight shining through branches of pine trees overhead; the sound of a night bird, someone calling from a long way off—where has she gone?

a man calling from a distance, wearing a ring on his finger, heavy as the rock where america lies, asleep on a rock as a girl, long hair hanging down, into the grass; a man who comes looking for her, hiking up the trail; does he call out her name, carry a lamp; does he lay wires across the trail to light this landscape where a young girl lies alone sleeping, does she wait for another point in time, to be carried to her like a grain of sand in a glass, or that is carried by an ocean wave, to a beach where she plays next to the water, building a sand castle, a bucket and shovel to collect the sand; she wades out a bit, into the ocean, into the waves, the floor of the sand firm beneath her as she steps and plants her feet, foamy white of the waves, soaking the blue cotton of her shorts and ribbons tied around her knees, as she leans into the water to look for a shell, for grains of sand that will form a castle on the beach; water over the sand that she pats with her hands; wading into the current, the water warm against her skin as it washes over her, under the sun that reflects off the waves and the sand of the beach where america runs, into the ocean, dropping beneath the water, before lifting her head and shaking it; or anastasia's husband holds her and she floats, a wave that carries her to the sandy beach where anastasia walks or sits underneath an umbrella watching robert and america; she lifts her skirts and wades out a bit, hand beneath the broad hat brim that shades her eyes from the sun; scooping sand up in the shovel or bucket, she makes a sand castle; america—a castle with turrets, a moat, a door, look: america, anastasia says, the tracks of a sea bird that walks along the shore, carrying food in a pink bill; a heron, a sea gull; anastasia points, listing out the names; and america listens, to the call of a gull; grey wings against the sand, a shell that america takes back to her room, listen: the sound of the surf in a shell, anastasia says, what do you think about that? that one day, the sound of ocean waves rising will recede; one day, under the confines of a skirt a young girl will swell, underneath the hand of a woman, a girl waiting to be born; before the first streaks of light cross a windowpane, step through a door and look at a child in anastasia's hands, opening her eyes at the sight of two people staring—

in this mountain meadow it is walker who stands, pulling a handkerchief from a pocket to wipe her eyes, it is anastasia who turns, hands america to robert and takes from her desk drawer a diary and she writes with a feather pen; a girl gazing out at the moon, carrying a walking stick through the fields where she walks in a skirt, down a trail, away from her home, a white house with black shutters set back from a dirt road, a town where anastasia teaches in the boarding school and robert lays down wires, across the land, beside a road; a train that runs through the town, whistling before it appears, the train that comes down the track and disappears into the trees where america runs as a girl, gathering flowers that she puts in her hat, wearing black boots and a long skirt; a row of buttons, a bow that she unties from her waist, when she takes off her skirt to bathe, hair flowing out beneath her hat as she runs her toes through the water, in the stream by the house where her family lives; does she sometimes stray away into the clearing, a bit far from the trail she is so familiar with, on a moonlit night, as she lies on a rock, sleeping beneath a tree, she won't be gone long, anastasia says, under a starry night, the full moon above, her parents worried and wondering about her, calling out her name—anastasia? walker turns around, wearing waders and carrying a fishing rod and creel, two fish that he has caught in the pond. he turns to look for natalia; anastasia, through the trees, as he whistles for his daughters—walker? over here—it is nadine who appears, carrying a fishing rod and creel, then natalia, from among the trees—natalia, walker says, you've been gone a long time—i was worried, you two, walking away from the trail—but we know this place, nadine says, we didn't get lost—we were picking flowers, hiking down the trail.

walker's footsteps echo against the cliff walls to accompany the singing of birds and the stream that flows beside them as they walk over rocks, through marshy ground, spongy beneath the hiking boots that natalia tied early in the morning, before going fishing on the trail; that morning, natalia had shaken nadine, it's five in the morning—not letting her rest as the sun came up, in the mist, over the lake by the tent they had pitched; water weighing down the flower heads in the meadow, purple and white; water shining on natalia's hiking boots as she walks through the grass, takes sticks from a pack and lights a fire where she and walker stand warming themselves until nadine crawls out from the tent, what's for breakfast? pancakes, natalia says, with blueberries that walker picked—nadine, you can mix them—natalia puts a pan on the fire as their mother sleeps; when she gets up to eat, i'm going hiking—nadine says, maybe I'll go with you—up that trail, celia points—natalia says, walker and i will go up the mountain—we can meet at the fork, natalia says, when the sun starts to set, we'll wait for you there—are you taking a fishing rod? yes—and something to put strawberries in, celia says, in case we find any on the trail. aren't you wearing long pants, nadine? i better, i guess—you're going to scrape your knees, and the plants and bushes are wet—you'll get soaked— that's why it's easier to wear a skirt, the water will dry against my skin. but it will be cold tonight—nadine shrugs, walks to the tent and comes out wearing a pair of blue jeans—celia, can you carry my skirt—celia bundles it up and puts it in her pack; then, i'm going to take some cheese. do you want cheese and crackers? walker says, yes, as the sun starts to rise over the lake, dispelling the mist that disappears over mountaintops, rises up from the flowers and grass, into the clouds—will it rain? the surface of the lake, smooth like glass, as natalia brushes her hair, washing her hands and neck, dipping her hands in the water and throwing it over her face—wake up, natalia—freezing cold—she sees her reflection in the water, nadine next to her—see how much we look alike—the reflection of your hair—in smooth waves down her back, like the ripple in the lake; a splashing sound as water falls from natalia's hands, on her face and into her reflection in the stream, rippling until it forms back again, the water holding still under the sight of two girls whose eyes focus on their reflections; walker asks, are we ready to go? upstream, up the trail through the trees, walker and celia, natalia and

nadine, above the lake that grows smaller as they climb the mountaintop—should we take the tent down tonight, below the pond?
yes—dirt and rocks rolling beneath their feet, look: at the flowers growing there—purple, an array of white—we'll gather them
in the meadow tonight, when we come back down the trail. hurry, nadine, natalia says as she leaves her behind, up the trail until
the path forks between two peaks—this way? nadine points, and
walker and natalia continue walking up the trail, waving at celia
and nadine, i can see her through the trees, there—walker thinks
of anastasia—we used to go hiking together, walker says, taking
natalia's hand; i don't need help to get across—no—it just reminds
me of the past, when you were young—sitting by the brook—as
they walk up the trail, until the sun shines high above them and
natalia sees a rock, i think i'll sit here—do you need waders, walker
asks—look, you can wade into the pool; water falling from a cliff
into the pool below and natalia thinks, i could float away, if i'd
like—i'm going to roll up my pants, and wade into the stream—is
it cold? yes—i'll put my waders on if my legs start to freeze—and
don't get sunburned—no—walker ties a fly on his line as natalia
ties on a lure and casts into the stream—can you see any fish in the
pool? there's a big one, look—i would hate to catch that one, natalia says, it's been living so long in this pool—floating by a rock, is
it asleep, natalia asks—but then walker steps into the stream, making a splashing sound, scaring the fish away—it's almost nine—we
should be heading back by five—that may be too early, for mother
and nadine—and you know you will want to stay until the sun has
almost set—but we should move camp, further down the trail. you
can come and get me, natalia says, when you're ready to go back—
i'll stay here; or whistle to you, if i go further up the trail.

beside the stream now, natalia puts on waders, casting her line,
tying a fly or singing a song, lying on a rock beneath a tree, looking
at the current of the stream, watching the birds fly above her or fish
swimming below; flowers and grass wave with the wind, sound of
the breeze through branches of pine trees, causing them to sway
above her, and creak; like the opening of a door, natalia thinks;
the sound of water running, like notes on piano keys that rise and

recede, the sound of ocean waves, white foam on the crest of a wave that carries a sound; a crimson dress blowing in the wind as a young girl walks, carrying a walking stick beside the stream where natalia sits, singing a song; the song of a woman whose eyes have turned from a city by a forest that grows around her; america, listening to the call of a bird, notes slow and held long as her father stands fishing, and she can hear the sound of his footstep rising up and echoing, in the distance, against the cliff walls or through the trees; she hears the sound of his fly rod as he whips the line up and lets it fall, into the water, over the rocky river bed where fish swim beneath the current; closing her eyes, she imagines him taking from his pocket a handkerchief, wiping his forehead or his glasses as he takes them from his eyes, does he drop them into the stream, look through the lenses to the distortions of plants and rocks beneath the water; does a fish look back at him before it swims away; does one swim toward walker now, fins and gills in barely perceptible motion; hold its gaze on walker, perch his glasses upon its nose; walker lifts the fish from the water, soft white belly smooth to the touch, the pink stripe of a rainbow on its side; walker puts the fish in his creel, to carry it back down the trail to where natalia sits, hearing his steps as he makes his approach; walker stops to fish—hearing the notes of the river current and natalia takes from her pocket a notebook and pen—

howdy, camper—howdy, stranger—i was writing down notes. like the brook makes—or the sound of the birds—feet—feet hitting the trail, and the sound rises up to echo—above the sound of the wind stirring branches of trees, disturbing rocks that begin to roll down the mountaintop, making a crashing sound where nadine and her mother stand now, high up on the trail—can you see them—no. they're standing there—walker points, not where the rocks are rolling down—to the right—nadine's wearing a red sweater—yes—and celia's dressed in white. they're coming down the mountaintop—look how fast they're walking. nadine, natalia says, never walks that fast when she's just with me—no? remember when i was a girl, and mother would go hiking with her, and we went fishing alone. maybe she's caught some fish—i only caught one, walker says—brook trout or a rainbow? rainbow, it has a big pink stripe. eyes that look out and up, or further still, down the trail; natalia pulls her hair up, under her hat—we should begin walking downhill—did you catch anything? no—i was writing down notes—remember when you used to say that nadine shouldn't get to eat anything, when she didn't catch fish—but she used to fix vegetables—you said that didn't count. because she would sit all day at camp, reading a book—i was writing down notes; then, natalia says, things were different, then—what? maybe i didn't know how to understand nadine—natalia calls, whistling through the trees, can she hear us yet—you two weren't so different, really—but the time is different now; a place in the meadow, remember—when you told me you weren't sure you could write down the notes—i'm still not sure that i know what i hear—in my sleep, or fishing by the brook— but you're writing now, and performing—yes.

a bouquet of flowers thrown over a banister, or onto a stage, where a woman stands, dressed in white—i feel, natalia says, as though i don't have any choice, hearing these sounds—walker stops to look at natalia, who stands behind him, a little bit above him on the trail. but you like what you do—walker says, think of your mother, working in an office, or me, working on homes. even your sister nadine says—the sound of notes, carried above an audience, eyes focused on her—even nadine says, the sounds make her feel—but that's because she's my sister; nadine, she calls—walker says, listen to me: one day, a woman's life will fade like the mist. walker says, natalia, are you listening to me? anastasia, who turns around to stare, like the woman wearing glasses, fishing from the director's chair as the sun starts to go down; celia says, nadine? natalia calls, is that you? they still can't hear us, walker says, look—at the lake below, reflecting the trees and mountains above—sound of feet down a trail, natalia? there you are, nadine. what are you doing now, nadine asks, as walker stares at the reflection on the lake of the trees. i'm trying to put the notes together—why don't we go gather flowers—by the side of the trail? yes—they look better over there. there's a patch of orange mushrooms, celia points—don't wander too far away, walker says, we need to eat dinner, and we have to move the tent—if we're going to get home early tomorrow—

is tomorrow sunday? yes—will we go before or after dinner— that depends how late we hike. here's two fish—nadine hands them to walker, why don't you clean them by the lake, while natalia and i gather wood. but i don't like cleaning them—no one does—nadine shrugs, next time we'll clean them; it will be our turn. did you learn how to clean them when i was gone from home? i always knew how—i just didn't want to. why would i, natalia—you didn't mind doing that. i used to think—what? nothing, nadine. eyes on her with pinpoint focus, like the stars; natalia says, of native american rituals, and catholicism—what do you mean? while i was cleaning the fish—closing of eyes; clear and dark, the water, the stream—walker doesn't like cleaning them—only hiking through the mountain meadows, going up a trail—i've never known how to ask him—what? natalia says, into the mist, the clear song of a woman singing, like ribbon bound to a hat—what was that? natalia looks—just a falling branch—it's getting dark—can you see. pick more flowers—or we'll have to help clean fish? i don't mean that, but we don't have enough for the vase—can you look—that's good, for now—walker and mother will be worried, if we don't start going back. are they waiting—down at the bottom—can you see them? over there—is that the trail now—yes—

our footsteps echo, even though the dirt is so soft. the woman gets up from the director's chair, taking the white visor from her head—that's our tent—where are celia and walker—down at the lake? maybe we should fold up the tent. are you sure? i don't want to put it up, if walker changes his mind. but he won't. tomorrow is sunday, and he'll have to get back to work. he might want to hike all day. i hope not. walker? your mother and i finished cleaning the fish, have you started the fire? he takes the fish from his creel and puts them down by the grate. that one's huge—natalia, is the wood dry enough? it didn't even rain—but it's wet—it will burn—throwing paper and wood on the grate, natalia lights the fire, do we have vegetables—i brought them—celia takes them from her pack. we saw you, up on the mountainside, we thought you looked like two dots. did you hear the rocks falling down? yes—it's a good thing you weren't in the boulder field. no, celia says, i knew not to go that way. are the fish almost done? that's no way to test them, nadine, with that stick—sorry—why do you do that, i've always told you—even when you were small—it's a matter of respect—

hush. walker stands from his rock and brings out paper plates, forks and knives; we have salad and bread—any salad dressing? no— are we taking the tent down? we'll have to carry the lamp—walker, through the trees, carrying a lamp and a pack; behind him, celia, natalia and nadine. was that enough fish? yes—tomorrow, i don't want to go back to work. neither do i—i don't mind, natalia says, practicing violin; composing music—you don't have a job, really— nadine—not like working in a bookstore, or putting in a floor—. but it's still work. down the trail swiftly now, natalia's hair flows out and it will tangle, so she tucks it under her hat. natalia? what? how far do we have to go—i don't know, nadine. it's dark—but at least it's not cold—hold the lamp higher—can you see? when do you want to go back home, natalia—i haven't decided yet—and she thinks, to stay here, to go camping, with my family, by the stream; the sounds that i hear, notes, running by the stream, notes, as natalia and nadine sit by the fireside, celia and walker setting up the tent and put- ting out sleeping bags; where are the flowers? here—set them in this— the water's cold—listen—to the running of the brook; the sad song of a woman singing in a meadow, alone, wiping with her apron her hands, drying her eyes, tears or mist; into the silence, now, as natalia is falling asleep—i keep hearing notes—like steam rising over the mountaintop, from the lakes to the clouds above, mist; under a street lamp, a man across the sidewalk, wearing white shoes, a circle of words, clear and dark on a melancholy note, leaves in the wind carried across a meadow, a message, through the trees, a girl whose hair is long, wearing a long dress and an apron, blue eyes open wide, across a sidewalk, under- neath the moon, rain from the sky that drops on the pavement where nadine stands beside the ocean, a red sweater and black skirt, a trolley car and nadine looks, at the red and green, into the future where some- one stands, wearing a suit; where are you going, natalia—as the clock chimes, natalia turns to walk down the sidewalk and someone walks between glass doors, down a corridor, white carpet spongy beneath his feet; a part on violin that natalia plays in a practice room; erika as she sings from the confines of a room, slow and hollow and long, natalia hears the cry of a bird overhead—or is it america, sitting up in bed, shading her eyes against the sunlight as anastasia opens the blinds, letting in light and the sound of a whippoorwill; anastasia, singing out notes, as america pulls on a dress and stockings, i'm going for a walk—

snow that falls from the sky, creating a blanket around america's hair and face; in this mountain meadow now it is a woman whose gaze turns to the future, away from the past, to a road that goes beyond the place where america gathers flowers that she will take to her mother and set in a vase; through the door, a man carrying a hat and hanging up a coat, laying down wires, across the fields where flowers are growing—the glare of sunlight on a lake or over ocean waves that crash against a boat, docked in the harbor on the shore where natalia sits, writing down notes—what was that sound? a woman, singing softly to herself; she puts down her pencil and sighs, stretches her arms to the sky before lying flat in the grass, hair blowing against the wind, obscuring from her view the sky and clouds above her, as the sun begins to set and she feels the spray of ocean water on her face, wind like fingers through hair or sounds that run through her head, in a dream; natalia picks up her notebook, a part for violin—sound of notes like wind through the trees, carried on an ocean current or by the river, from a place natalia cannot see, surrounded by darkness, a voice calling in the mist, natalia—

natalia turns around, in a dream, standing on the sidewalk, under the moon, ocean waves carrying sand to america, a girl who picks up a hatpin, a pearl, a straw hat, ribbon bound around the rim; a snake coiled, lying on a rock; notes coiling through the trees, where america sits, under a black hat, in black and white photographs on the piano, gold frames, hair tumbling out beneath a hat as natalia hands someone a glass and turns, and she thinks, i might as well drop out of school, go fishing, find a cabin in the woods, beyond the place where traffic sounds heavy as thunder rolling through the hills, where natalia walked as a girl—natalia, wake up—natalia walks to the door to let heath in; i was dreaming—; you're always dreaming, heath says, you're late—throws her a sweater and pair of black pants, here—natalia looks; i thought you didn't care what you wear—not like nadine, natalia says; then, she might come visit me; or maybe i'll go there—don't miss school to do it—i dreamed i was tending bar, last night. just don't drop out of school, heath says. why would i do that? i don't know, heath says, the way you daydream in class, always looking out the window—what are you thinking about—notes—in the confines of a room—see that picture—that woman wearing a hat. when i was young, natalia says, i used to want to write down sounds like i heard in the meadow, sitting by the brook—

underneath the moon, cacophony of voices, the dissonant sound of a plane engine, across the sky, tires screeching against the pavement; a woman who looks down the runway, lights pointing like stars, a spotlight like a cone where a woman stands in a red dress, collecting flowers from a stage like leaves; red petals across the floor where the orchestra members walk, across white tiles, picking up their instruments to the strike of a baton; a woman who looks at an audience, eyes focused on her; carry me across; above a stream running over a mountaintop where she once ran as a girl—america—in a white dress, down a dark aisle, a woman scattering petals like leaves—someone who lights a candle; does she begin to pray, against the black night that enfolds her; or is she only writing down notes, gold or brass, on the keys of an instrument, a piano in a church as she imagines playing as a girl, natalia—i'm coming, heath; we have a history test—and natalia thinks, i don't have time—what if i ever met someone, heath—what do you mean? rain against the glass, falling from the sky and streaking the windowpanes of the classroom; what about dan? he still wants me to live with him— maybe just for the sake of having me there—into the future, look: at the river winding through the trees, natalia, what do you think of that? what? natalia looks up at her teacher now, what did you ask? if one day, a woman's life would fade in the mist—i don't know the answer to that. heath looks at her as natalia looks down and heath says, you weren't listening—but i was hearing these notes—natalia points, black against green, we can play them out, later on. what does that mean— natalia—you're not paying attention again—down the hall, out on the street natalia hears footsteps fading away, you'll have to study harder than that, and pay attention in class—what about your scholarship?

glow of a streetlight where heath stands, waiting for her—can you play this part on violin—heath plays the melody, and natalia says, it's better to write the notes than pay attention in class—i don't think they're asking that much—that's what nadine says—what is she doing now? working in the bookstore; she may go somewhere else—

across the mountain meadow, not so far away, natalia thinks as she runs water for a bath, soaps her hair and rinses it, i wonder what walker is doing now; anastasia by the light of a lamp, hair falling around her shoulders as america lies, asleep, anastasia, taking from her desk a diary and pen; erika asks, why don't you write for a quintet—a symphony—a woman's voice above violins, clear and hollow and long, the sound of a nightingale as anastasia closes her eyes to sleep—maybe if i wasn't in school, natalia says, we could play in a chamber group. heath says, you'd have to play piano—i'm playing violin. i'm not good enough—a woman whose eyes are on a girl, in a mirror or in the reflection of a pool in a stream; natalia asks heath, where are you going? i have to practice violin; and natalia sits in her room, thinking about the flowers she will pick in springtime, when she goes home again; walker, sitting in a chair, turning on a light to read a letter from natalia; the picture of two girls, standing in a meadow holding flowers in their arms; does a dark night sky enfold them like wings, a man in a black robe who sings or a woman dressed in white, counting out notes as pages turn, the turn of a clock, hands around the center, and natalia looks out the window, down the steps where heath walks, be here before nine—the sounds of the street fade as natalia turns out her light, notes, the sounds of a dream—a man on the sidewalk; heath says, he must be waiting for you—i don't think he'd bother to do that—across the street, under the moon, a voice from the past that comes in clear notes, a song, a diary, a book that someone puts down in his lap, watching natalia read, across the sky, clouds that form above the trail where walker stands, hands on his hips and gazing into the mist at the mountain peak that celia climbs, by herself; nadine, on a street where the hills climb from the ocean, through the fog, a woman standing in a crimson dress with white lace and black stockings, a black hat and bobbed hair, america—where can she have gone—

across the meadow, away from the mountains and trees, a frame house in the woods, bathing her feet and running her toes through the sand until anastasia picks her up and carries her, across the beach, through time where a sound is waiting to be heard, through the silence, the chime of a triangle or a dull screaming that natalia hears, nadine covering her ears; don't, nadine says, practice now—; out of the house to the church where natalia played as a girl, below the stained glass windows falls the light mist of rain, glowing beneath a street lamp as natalia practices in a church where no one is now; notes echoing above her like the sound of thunder, rain, as natalia walks home; in a deep sleep, words whispered through a dream, sunlight between window blinds casting a crooked shadow across the floor where natalia steps through papers scattered like leaves, a rough whispering, paper scratching, across strings, a table and a vase full of cut flowers from a meadow; into a brook, falling, leaves, as the sun goes behind the clouds and walker waits as leaves turn and the sun comes between the trees, he walks downhill, two fish in his creel that he has caught; natalia—walker looks; but it is only a percussive echoing, feet against a trail or a whippoorwill's song carried on the wind. walker hears the hollow sound of his footsteps now; feet, hitting the trail, and he looks through the branches of trees standing high overhead, but he cannot think nor imagine what natalia might be doing, walking with heath down a sidewalk, carrying a violin; two percussive sounds as natalia snaps her violin case shut, wearing a black tuxedo, red suspenders and a black bow tie, her hair tied behind her head; across the stage, red petals scattered like leaves, natalia holding a bunch of flowers in her arms—

across the meadow, a voice that sings, a melody on violins, a flute; erika as she sings under a spotlight, dark skin and a white dress, gold of a harp, brass, a flute, a percussive echoing as natalia snaps her violin case shut, down the black pavement wearing white shoes; erika says, where should we go—heath says, i have a new recording—as the music plays and heath brings out glasses, what are you going to write now? i don't know, natalia says—your pieces have become more complicated—that's what nadine said in her letter—walking to work down a black street in a red skirt, green of a trolley car rolling by under the rain, through the fog, mist, car horns, taxi tires rolling smooth as a sailing ship, under the streetlights, the light of a lamp where natalia works, hands across the face of a clock, misty glow in the rain and there walker stands, wearing waders and a fishing vest, tying a fly, or walking, further still, down the trail, can you see, dear reader, his hair rippling gently in the wind as he thinks about a girl who once wore waders and a fishing vest, tucking her hair under her cap, casting a line into the brook as the bubble falls, making a whipping noise as she pulls the fly up from the water or the bough of a pine tree where it has caught; singing softly to herself when the sun comes from behind the clouds to slant through the branches of trees; or natalia's face and hair, over her reflection as she sits, a drop into the stream, into the brook—a tear that falls, fabric fraying, a tear in the fabric and anastasia picks up the pieces, we can fix this, i guess—america— you shouldn't go running through the woods, wearing dark stockings and a dress—a woman walking up the trail, lying down beside a rock where she slept—a tear in the fabric; anastasia lifting her skirts to walk, a dress that tears, pulled apart at the seams, branches that will catch, through the weeds, on a rock, fabric cut and fraying, or sewn up in the confines of a room, a dress that will catch in the wind, or tear, when the angle is right—underneath a hat, long hair falling down—voices across the stream, america—where has she gone? running through the woods or across a beach, running her toes through the sand, lifting up skirts over weeds, lifting the hem, cutting her hair, wearing bobbed hair and a black hat, black hair and blue eyes, in the silver frame of a picture that natalia keeps on the piano—can you listen to this— heath puts his violin down, what was that sound? one day, a woman's life will fade in the mist—on a dark night, starry sky surrounding her, mere pinpoints of light focused on erika as she sings in a black dress, clack of quick heels across white tiles, rustle of pages that turn, the violins; this part in three-eight, the next part in four-four—a sigh above the instruments, carry me across, to another point in time, across the ocean, across the waves, smooth as a sailing ship, when no sun shines through the trees; we can't have another rehearsal of this—does natalia hold her head in her hands; a voice that is fading, the wail of sirens above traffic, a hand that is flashing, signaling to stop—a man walking across the pavement holding a brief case in his hand—haven't i seen you before—playing pieces in the light of a room—on harp, a part for percussion instruments; clear as that woman sitting, fishing, beside a pond, wearing a white cotton visor on her head, plants lining the bottom of the pond—something growing here—natalia looks down at her dress; america—walker asks, natalia, do you remember when we used to go fishing—sitting, from the director's chairs—where a girl once stood, singing, carrying a walking stick, a bundle of flowers or a girl, under the confines of a skirt, in the rain and there someone stands who once stood beside a stream, fishing, or under a street lamp, waiting for a subway, walking in the rain, carrying an umbrella and holding a newspaper as he walked; did he listen to the sound of a whippoorwill, or a girl singing softly to herself, on a train; wheels around the center as the tracks disappear, underneath these wheels—

america, pulling on white stockings and black shoes, a blue dress that will tear above the weeds, if she doesn't lift her skirt over the grass as she steps, above the rocks, across the stream, the clear sound of water running—a dress sewn together, america—you should lift your skirt when you walk—but i can't, when i am thinking of something—walking through the meadow, looking at the trees—your great-grandmother, anastasia says, wouldn't have been allowed to go out alone—under a starry night, the full moon above—is someone calling out her name— had she gotten lost, did everyone worry this time, for good—or was she only hiding from the light that fell from above, covering her head with her hat, or stopping by a stream, cupping her hands to drink, staring at her reflection in the glass, it is anastasia brushing out her hair— you'll have to go walking in something else—a dress turned up, or sewn at the seams—a girl in a picture frame, bobbed curls and a black hat, wandering through the woods, putting a worm on a hook—the woman in the director's chair looks at walker now, wearing dark glasses to shield her eyes from the sun, or from a gaze that would carry the weight of a river current, that would carry her further into the future, shading her eyes with a hand against the bright sunlight, calling out someone's name, in a mountain meadow, anastasia, wiping with her apron her hands, as walker lowers his glasses from his eyes, does the woman in the director's chair stand, against the wind that is blowing the white cotton visor from her head, wind like fingers through hair, brushing hair like leaves, across the sidewalk, scattered and blowing, comes the sound of notes on horns, the sound of someone's approach, rough as the scratch of paper against strings, the notes on violin—carry me across—

walker looks at anastasia now; what can she be thinking, dear reader, as she stands alone, gazing into the abyss—notes, scattering like dust or a light rain; words from lips, silhouette, wafting up and then floating gently down, the words of a man or notes on violin that natalia plays, in front of the orchestra, a cone of light that enfolds her, white robes, angels' wings, taking her beyond the abyss, a bridge; span of wires, the sound of instruments lifting the emotions of a girl who sings, the song of a woman, when the moon shines from above, so that she can see to write words across a page with a black feather pen—anastasia puts her diary down, smoothes the quilt on the bed where america lies, asleep—carried to her like a grain of sand on an ocean current, someone who tore her skirt, buttoning her dress; the blue one is too tight, i think—anastasia, pulling back america's hair—just don't go walking alone, too far; or running through the weeds—walker puts the letter he is reading down, in the living room; in the frame of a picture, a girl wearing waders, dark curls—another girl who sits reading a book, wearing a dress; is she doing well in school—well enough to pass—

by the stream where walker fishes by the light of a lamp, after the sun has gone down; clouds, a voice in the mist—the reflection of a woman or a girl in the pool beneath his feet that ripples when he steps, causing the fish in the pool to swim a little bit away—walker casts his line into the brook as the fish rise, whips the line up before letting it float gently into the stream, a fish that looks at him and swims away—in this mountain meadow walker stands, his fishing creel empty and he steps, carrying the lamp and his fishing rod, across the rocks, across the brook, i used to carry you—but there is no voice from behind; only the sound of wind through the trees, birds that sing; feet, against the trail, the hollow sound of feet echoing, the ground spongy and soft beneath his feet as walker hums softly, gathering flowers, he thinks to himself, pink and purple, an array of white, the notes that natalia sings to herself before writing them down; heath? it's time to get up—natalia calls him from the sidewalk in the morning, i think we should practice this— yes—i don't have time, to practice and write—i'm getting less sleep; i never slept much as a girl—looking at the stained glass windows, are you listening to me?

anastasia, writing in a diary, writing down her thoughts; wearing long skirts, asleep on a rock, her parents worried, was she lost—until the sun came up over the mountaintops, through the mist—america—a girl who pulled her skirts up, when the length was so long, yards of fabric cut and sewn into a dress, tearing, streaks of rain running down a windowpane where anastasia looked out at the night sky, as a girl—america—the sun through a windowpane where she lies, opening her eyes, under white sheets and a patchwork quilt, touching her toes to the wood floor, splashing water on her face, she closes her eyes, soaps and washes, dries her face before putting on a dress—we should pin this up—anastasia takes pins from a cushion, we can fix that, i guess—but you shouldn't go running through the weeds—down the steps, holding a fishing rod and a white straw hat; she looks at the stream, flowing beside her; digging a worm from the can, she folds it and puts it on the hook, beneath a tree, she closes her eyes, singing softly to herself, until the line pulls, and she pulls the fish from the stream; hitting the fish hard, on the head, causes america to shake, a little bit—but she picks the fish up, carrying it downhill, looking at the flowers growing and she thinks to gather a bunch, to put in a vase; flowers that she folds in her apron, that she can take down the trail to where anastasia is waiting for her—you weren't gone so long— i already caught a fish—anastasia stands from the table, she slits the fish belly as america closes her eyes; he won't mind that i went fishing—no—only when you get lost—but i'm never lost—when you stay out, anastasia says, longer than you should. i'm going back inside—does america sit down and cry, or shade her eyes to see— anastasia, cleaning a fish—when i was young, i would watch my father, fishing by the brook; over a fire, anastasia throws the fish; i brought flowers from the meadow, can we put them in a vase—as the sun begins to set, your father will come back soon—

across the meadow, a light that is fading, steps across the floor; america's father sits down, by the light of the candle, you weren't gone too long—and you didn't tear your dress—sitting under a tree, a man in the mist; a man whose daughter is growing, beneath the confines of a skirt—the reflection of a woman as she takes down pins from her hair, carrying a hat and flowers, and in a bundle of blankets, a girl; steps on a stair, descending into the auditorium, under bright lights a woman who sings, does she raise her arms to the sky, toward a white robe that will enfold her; lifting her skirts over weeds, does she fold her hands, in a church, under the stained glass window, is she kneeling down to pray, to break the silence that surrounds her, creating notes, in a black jacket and white shirt, wearing white shoes, does she write a melody for voices, in the silence of the auditorium, rising above the audience, in a whirlwind like leaves, papers blowing, notes into memory, into the past, someone who walks down a trail singing a tune, wearing a hat and holding her hand, a girl beneath the sunlight, singing a song she has learned at school, a melody from a time in the past that fades; into the present, now, it is a woman who looks, at a stream or a written line of notes, green disappearing into black as natalia writes the pieces she hears in her sleep, that come to her as though across the meadow, through the trees where someone steps; it is anastasia, taking off dark glasses it is the woman who turns around, natalia, i'm getting behind—walker taking nadine's hand as she steps across the brook; a melancholy accompaniment—i should never have left this place, natalia thinks; a place far from my childhood that has disappeared in the mist, even from my memory, the past disappears behind, underneath these wheels—a man disappeared from my midst, gold into black; the sounds of a city fading from natalia's memory so that she cannot envision, cannot think nor imagine what dan might be doing, across an ocean, a harbor, boats; casting a line into the stream, dear reader, what can you be thinking as natalia disappears, wearing a cap and carrying a fishing rod, as she hikes down the trail, hair flowing out beneath her hat; on the path that sinks slightly, underneath her feet, spongy soft ground, under the moon that has not yet set, natalia looks into the trees, before whistling—natalia—the sound under a streetlight fading, like the place where natalia stands, the ground shifting beneath her feet, does she fall into the abyss—

heath, calling natalia—underneath a spotlight, on the sidewalk comes the tread of footsteps, on a stair, natalia, wake up—i was dreaming—walking in the mountain meadow—but no one was there—the sound of a whippoorwill, to accompany the sound of the running brook—feet, down a trail, the sound of footsteps that echo, carried across on an ocean current, a grain of sand into a woman's palm, a pearl; america, singing softly to herself, the sound of a woman's feelings as a man walks away, leaving her behind; natalia—you wanted to leave, heath says, you couldn't have kept living there, with dan—natalia sits down and cries, in the apartment where she is living, alone—and now you are free of the past—green into black; purple flowers, an array of white, gold and yellow; an abyss and natalia says, look, nadine: anastasia, running through the woods, carrying a child or a bundle of flowers; a gold band on a finger, an engagement ring, in the black and white of a photograph, wearing a white gown or a black dress, a wreath of flowers as she walks between aisles, beneath the stained glass, toward arms that enfold her; a man in a black suit wearing a white tie, carry me across—to a time that cannot be seen yet; into the future, even if you look, you cannot know the complications and twists, the sights further up a trail, down an aisle, through the streets, someone walking, wearing white shoes, down an avenue and into a practice room; women's voices, violins, natalia at the podium, closing her eyes—but she cannot think nor imagine what dan might be doing, in another city, or walking down a trail where walker stands, voices of women singing, it is walker who hears them as natalia walks, up the hill to her apartment, writing as heath practices violin and erika sings, in the dark of a practice room; walking up a hill, nadine, standing under the moon—the whistle of a tea kettle, steam streaking down the windowpane, drops forming from the mist, rising high above natalia, into the clouds against the blue sky where walker shakes a stone from his shoe; putting it back on, he laces it, before shading his eyes against the sun, wearing a hat, arms that enfold him— natalia, nadine—not so far away—a memory, as the future takes shape, created against a background of women's voices, singing quietly as the violins play; i'm not sure i like the sound of that, heath says; it's just that it's unusual, and you're not used to it yet—erika, in a black dress with a gold band around her neck, wearing gold shoes on a white tiled floor in front of women wearing white gowns as they sing—softly, natalia says, the piano accompaniment—

nadine looks at the red velvet seats; i am not one to walk so slowly—close the shutters—the light across the street—another place, not so fraught with memory even as the past disappears, beneath these wheels, dust stirring, mere particles in the air—two notes stirring ashes of a fire; coals that spark before they are lit, bursting into flame, the sound of a refrain, in the meadow where anastasia looks up at the night sky, stars shining with pinpoint focus on her, drops like mist, rain that falls from clouds that form above a stream of notes that carries the emotions of a girl, like a tear that falls into a puddle, making a splash and scaring the fish away, carried to an ocean current where the waves wash up sand to the shore, where someone waits, holding a straw hat in her hand; what is she looking for, wearing dark glasses under the rain when no sun shines through the trees—is there something of the silence where someone stands waiting for something, is he looking for a girl carrying a hat and walking stick; anastasia, a pearl that she finds by the ocean, washed up on this beach, in a shell; is she thinking about the past as it flows by her, carried as though by the river current, to a place where natalia stands listening to the sound of the stream that flows by her, traffic that goes below, beneath the wheels, as it starts to rain, in a clearing in the mountains; beneath a bridge, the still of a river current as natalia walks, wearing a suit coat and carrying a violin, down the street wearing white shoes, into the silence, now, it is after the fact, as someone disappears from hawkes point to north point, beyond the place where a woman walks down an aisle wearing a white gown, in a church, natalia closes her eyes to hear the sounds of the instruments; a man in the meadow never questioning his world, wind stirring a melody like a dress that blows against the breeze as america walks, does she wear a gold ring, black curls and a black hat, mittens to keep her hands warm until she writes a letter to a man, words across a page, a hand signaling to stop as natalia walks with heath, to the apartment where natalia writes a part for violin, a solo that heath plays in a black suit and bow tie; notes carried to the city where nadine works, in a bookstore, neon lights glowing; writing a letter, across the miles, a man who waits—america—where can she have gone?

swinging a hat under the full moon that shines down like a cone of light, falling, closing her eyes, natalia, holding a bundle of flowers in her hands, america turns to see, the sound of water falling, thunder that claps and is gone, a flash of lightning that illuminates the trail where america walks, more quickly now as the storm begins, rain falling over her shoulders and hair, mud on her feet, your boots—anastasia unties them as america shakes out her hair—you shouldn't have been gone so long—one day, a woman's life will fade, like the sight of a woman in a picture, or the sound on a phonograph, a piece performed in a city beyond the place where natalia lives; as she walks down an aisle, the hall of a music building, or the aisle between seats on an airplane that will carry her, as the past disappears beneath her, the ground sinks below, a city whose lights fade as the airplane carries her, like a grain of sand that falls from the hand of a man, a hatpin, a pearl; a ring that america wears on her finger in a picture that natalia keeps, above the piano as heath plays violin—look, natalia: at the sound of an instrument fading, a man walking underneath the streetlight who looks to the light through natalia's window—as the music plays and women sing, notes written by a girl who once stood in a stream, fishing, three bracelets on her arm, a sound to accompany the birds that sing in the trees high above her, notes of the brook, on violin—a man who waits for a girl, holding a hat as she walks down a flight of stairs or up an aisle, as a man speaks in a black robe, beneath a cross where a man waits, as though suspended on the wind, the thoughts of a man who writes a letter with a black pen on white paper, notes carried across the miles to a woman waiting for him; america—he may never come back—

an engagement ring in the folds of a letter; does america begin to cry; drinking a bottle of coke, shared demise; walker looks at natalia's mother across a white table, wearing glasses to shield his eyes; natalia says, the lights are too bright—as the orchestra plays, a part on violin, percussion instruments like thunder rolling through the hills where america walks holding a boy in her arms; walker—after his father, america says; she puts the letter she is writing down; sound of a door opening, the sound of feet up steps or a woman walking down an aisle wearing a white dress and holding a bundle of flowers, as she steps into the arms that will enfold her, in the future, america, as the past disappears, underneath these wheels, dust rising in a cloud, particles in the wind glowing bright against the sun, the straw of a white hat with ribbon bound around the rim, music that swings as america turns across the floor, pulled by the hand of a man as though by a river current; i won't be gone long—from the mountain meadow, over the hills, on a road laid down by a man like a track once laid down by a boy, through the fields, as anastasia sat on a rock, brushing out her hair, tying it up, writing a letter across the miles, walker says, look—a railroad track, as anastasia holds his hand and they walk down a trail; over a road as the dust rises beneath wheels, under the streetlights, the lights of the city—

an electrician, laying down wires, across a city; a house where anastasia hangs pictures and curtains, looking out the window at the ocean, away from the city where natalia lives, in the mountains, as a girl; america cries out, waiting to be heard—a sound carried to another place, in the distance, a foghorn, chime of a clock on a mantle, hands across the center, shatter of glass and a woman stands underneath a spotlight on stage, wearing a red dress and a gold band around her finger as the orchestra plays; a diamond weighing heavy as a weight of lead, the rock where anastasia laid down as a girl, against a tree, hair blowing against the wind, does walker shade his eyes, against the sun shining brightly on the woman in the director's chair, who wears dark glasses to shade her eyes, a woman who looks beyond where walker stands, above the timberline, to the barren land covered only with rock; the man sitting next to her gets up from the director's chair, taking a white cotton visor from his head, holding it in his hand, sipping from a glass of iced tea, he stares into the distance at anastasia wearing a long dress and a straw hat; with no reason to shade her eyes against the sunlight, does she begin to understand that a man in the meadow never questioning his world will walk down a trail carrying a fishing rod and creel; that a woman sitting in the director's chair will turn, at the sight of a woman whose gaze accompanies the notes written in natalia's apartment, from a time in the past that she cannot remember; she cannot think nor imagine how this place might have been, where so many people have stood across the land; a militiaman on a horse, holding reins in his hands, gazing across the hills to a street where natalia walks, holding the hand of a man, carry me across—to another place; not so young, natalia thinks, at this time; the voice of a girl that echoes against the hills, america, singing quietly to herself, across a bridge, a span of gold wires like harp strings as the instruments play in an auditorium, in the future, and natalia thinks about a time before she was born, when america sat at a desk writing a letter to a man in a uniform, waiting for him to come back—walking down a trail by the school where anastasia once taught; america gazes out the window at the flowers and trees in the meadow, looking into the glass, america, long hair flowing in smooth waves down her back, clear as an ocean current; a letter carried in a bottle, across the ocean, a man wearing a uniform, a picture that natalia keeps on the piano as she plays; america, writing letters to a man who has been sent away; drinking a bottle of coke, shared demise; walker says, i won't be gone long—

does he hold natalia's mother in his arms, a woman who emerges from a bundle in someone's arms, as she grows into a girl walking by the ocean, leaving footprints in the sand like the gulls that fly above her; at the sound of a foghorn blowing, america looks up and points, anastasia, the sound of a gull, against the sky as america draws the clouds above her, full as the skirt anastasia wears, walking across the sand, a woman with a parasol that shades her from the sun—don't be gone too long, america—studying flowers in the meadow, america writes down the names—she sits against a tree, holding a hat in her hand, until the line pulls and she wades into the water, moving away from the river bank, america holds the line in her hand, pulling the fish to the bank beside her; hitting the fish hard, on the head, causes america to shake a little bit—but anastasia will clean them; pulling a worm from a can that she puts on the hook, she casts the line into the water and sits beneath a tree; what can she be wondering, as she picks up the hat lying beside her and places it on her head; waiting, she thinks, as the sun has not gone down—until another fish bites at the line; taking it off the hook, carrying two fish and her fishing rod, she walks down the trail, happy that the sun has not yet set: earlier, the sun shone down warm, but now the sky is cloudy and the air cool, as thunder rumbles through the hills and anastasia looks out the window, i hope she'll come back soon—it's dark, and a storm seems to be coming—light a candle in the window for her.

america picks out a bunch of flowers, singing a tune to accompany the rain coming down, cold through the clothes she has worn: earlier that morning, america had said, i think i'll wear father's trousers—but they don't look good on you—i can't walk in a dress. i always did, anastasia says—did she never tear the fabric—cut and fraying, across the lines—a man who is waiting, carried like a message across an ocean current, to a woman who wears a black hat, who cut her hair, when the length was so long that she would get headaches whenever she looked into the glass; sharing a bottle of coke, i'll have to think about that, walker says; does natalia's mother sigh—a row of desks, across the page with a pen america writes the names of trees; drawing a picture, she labels the fish; natalia, putting her notebook down; the sound of these notes will only fade, into the silence, where they came from; or across the miles, nadine writes to natalia, you could come visit me; rolling hills and trolley cars, pavement that shines beneath her feet in the fog as natalia walks up the street and someone plays on saxophone, outside a cafe, green awning overhead—clack of heels against a cement walk, a woman who sings above the piano, creating a sound that is carried by the hands of a clock that spins above natalia; or is it something she cannot see nor begin to understand, under a clock, shatter of glass, a picture sitting, still on a piano where she works; sound of footsteps across white tiles, a woman wearing a gold band that natalia kept by america's picture, when she was a girl—

walker, in a uniform, gazing at the mountains that surround him, this is where i will live; does natalia's mother sit down and cry; a dress held up over weeds as she walks across the mountains and hills, the rivers flowing into the distance, away from the past—into the future, now, it is after the fact, riding a bus to hawkes point, to north point, to another place in time, where walker stands as a house is built—here is where we will stay, he thinks—across the fields, across the grass—anastasia turns and is gone, wearing long skirts and carrying a walking stick, a straw hat that blows against the wind, ribbon tight around the rim, like a snake that slithers into the dark, through the trees where anastasia disappears, into the black night that enfolds her, as the past disappears behind, stars that glow above natalia as she stands on a street corner singing notes, through the trees, a girl who once stood wearing waders and fishing in a stream—america—

taking a ring from the folds of a letter that she slips on her finger, string or twine—a ring on a finger; i don't think you should wait, anastasia says—; anastasia's diary, locked up in a desk—does someone pick it up to see—the story of a woman who ran through the fields, carrying a walking stick and holding a hat, giving birth to a girl; lying on a rock, long hair falling into the grass; her sister, who cut her hair when the length was so long, into the glass, hair tangling around her head, or coiled in a mass; a hatpin, a pearl on the hat that anastasia wears, given to her by a man, an electrician, laying down wires, living in a city, not so far away—laying down wires across the land, arriving on a train in the town where anastasia lives, lights across the city, in the school where anastasia teaches, a row of books across desks, blank pages covered with black; this is not how these letters should look, anastasia says; black feather pen across a page, in the diary that anastasia keeps, writing about a man—one day, rebecca says, you will end up all alone—words that are created, notes, cast in stone; like a line cast into a stream—i don't mind waiting—look. i think the water is too high—does someone pick her up and carry her, into his arms; or is it only the sight of anastasia's picture; i wonder what she was thinking about, natalia says to nadine, teaching in the boarding school—notes across the lines, a man laying down wires in the town where anastasia lives; the lights across the city—can we put these in a vase? flowers thrown over a banister or across a stage, petals, roses, red velvet seats; up an aisle, i won't walk across—traditions that enfold america, in smooth waves, surrounding her, the sound of silence until the reverberations of strains of notes are heard in the night, a discordant sound, ellen taaffe zwilich, paper clips between strings; sarah vaughan, nat king cole, stockhausen on a music box— grażyna bacewicz, samuel barber, in the confines of a practice room; dan, dancing across a stage in black tights as natalia watches, i didn't think we would grow apart—that we could create so much distance, dan says, in this time—

erika, in a black dress as she sings over the percussion instruments, above an audience, steam, drops into mist, disappearing in a cacophony of sound, footsteps on a stair, the turning of a lock, a man holding a bundle of red roses in his arms, petals thrown across a stage, a man at the podium who speaks words carried across an audience, to a girl who looks at the stained glass windows, suspended like words upon the air that hover above her, sounds floating as though on the wind, angels with wingtips, carried beyond a woman who sings in a black dress, wearing a gold band around her neck, dark skin like silk, a rustling sound in the audience, the turning of a page, rattle of bows against instruments as natalia picks up her baton, closing her eyes to count the notes as they are about to begin, at the piano as natalia plays and erika sings, notes across the sky like clouds that float above her—does someone look under the neon lights reflecting off the windowpane, through the glass, beyond the image floating, at natalia as she sits at a table, does he see the shadow of a woman fading—

a woman carried through the air by a plane or steps down a trail, down an aisle, between red velvet seats, the gold of an opera glass, eyes focused on a woman in white, rustle of a silk gown above pages that turn, tap of a bow against a violin; a woman holding a bouquet of flowers thrown above an audience, petals, steam, running down a windowpane, in drops on the glass, like tears streaking against a face, behind the glasses that walker wears, does he begin to cry, at the sight of natalia fading, walking across the pavement, wearing white shoes, a girl who once wore waders, casting a line into a stream; gaze beyond the glass, where dust falls like rain above a dirt road as the past disappears underneath these wheels, a whisper carried on the ocean current, a hatpin or a pearl, louise talma, stockhausen on a music box that plays as a ballet dancer turns to gaze into the glass, at the clear reflection of a meadow, in the water, look—beyond the mosaic fallen to the ground, beneath feet, into the abyss, notes running, carried to a girl; america—what can she be thinking, swimming so far out, into the waves—

a woman in a white gown shading her eyes against the reflection of the sun that falls, bouncing off the ocean waves, a girl beyond the shore, holding a beach ball in her hands, floating to where her father sits, waiting for her—america—when will she come back—from the place where a letter has been sent across the ocean, by a harbor where boats come in, a meadow, mountains, trees—can you see into the past, dear reader, to the place where a woman looks, into the mirror at a wedding dress, a band of gold smooth as silk, reflecting the sun that shines on it like a pair of glasses; drinking a bottle of coke, in a uniform, across the continent, beyond the place where he was born, gazing into the trees, as he walks up the trail, it is walker who reflects about the past, carrying a fishing rod and creel or leaning against a tree to put his waders on, to carry his fishing rod into the middle of the stream, making a splashing sound as he slips against the rocks; but he doesn't fall down, nor does he hit his head: tying a fly, holding the line between his teeth, he pulls the knot, casting into the stream, letting the fly float gently downward, the line making a whipping sound against the wind as the sun is beginning to set, and walker wades to the bank, walking in his waders down the trail, alone—does anastasia turn, in the meadow, as natalia reads the words written in her diary, from the point of a pen, black ink across a page, the life of a woman who went walking through the woods, carrying a walking stick and lifting her skirts over the weeds so that she will not fall into the grass, will not disappear into the abyss; what is that? a gold band—natalia walks down the steps, out the door, and she feels like covering her ears—even if we have to wait— anastasia's picture on the piano, eyes focused on her; a featherbed, a quilt that anastasia makes, patches sewn together; natalia sits on the edge of her bed, holding her head in her hands, drying her eyes to look out the window at the rain falling on the pavement, to the traffic that goes by in a stream, water falling, under the wheels, a puddle that reflects neon lights, lights of the street lamps and rain, natalia thinks, like tears as she walks through the city, rustle of leaves across the sidewalk, blowing above a churchyard, gusting into the air and then falling softly down, creating a blanket over the grass—a cord, like silk, a snake slithering into the woods, crawling over the grass, coiled on a rock like the braid in anastasia's hair that she ties on her head, walking down an aisle in a white gown, full skirts that rustle, slowly, and the piano carries a melancholy accompaniment through the aisles, above the pages of notes that an audience turns, white printed on black, written by a girl—does it make a difference now, who wrote these notes across a line—or is it the sound that is carried—like the letters of a man who writes to america—anastasia says, i'm sure he'll come home—a ring, string or twine—

a locomotive, steam; a suitcase shut tight; natalia waves to heath, by the tracks of a train—what happened to engineering, nadine—engineering or math—some people enjoy doing that—; walker says, i thought you did—because of natalia, always practicing those instruments—those same pieces over again, and the hard parts, when she was out of tune, or playing wrong notes—i'm sorry, nadine. and the notes could be heard everywhere—upstairs and down—that's why i took ballet, and i played in the church—listening to recordings, or whistling; singing before we went to sleep—if you hadn't shared a room—nadine shrugs, i would have heard her through the walls—but i don't mind listening now, it isn't just practicing—hearing the music you write—notes across a line, another place in time, clear as that woman sitting and wearing a hat—nadine stands up from her chair, i'm going to sleep now—fishing—we'll go next week—anastasia's picture, on top of the piano—don't play any more tonight, natalia—i'm just looking at her—eyes focused on a woman in a picture; she looks like you, walker says, you look like my grandmother, more than anyone—

aren't you glad i kept playing when i was young, nadine—that was a long time ago.

a memory, anastasia; does the woman in the director's chair turn, at the sight of two girls walking up stairs, red carpet that sinks slightly beneath their feet, as they walk away; natalia, up stairs and through the door where she hears the sound of a recording; heath—wake up. i was dreaming—a man in the meadow, never questioning his world—what was that? that sound—carried by a stream, like that woman sitting and wearing a hat, as she stands from the director's chair, at the sound of a rough whispering; is it only a percussive echoing, the sound of footsteps down stairs; looking from the window, green awning overhead; erika—heath says, we should be practicing today—taxi horns above the screech of tires on pavement, up steps and through a glass door, sound of instruments playing, natalia looks into a practice room, i wish i could write something like that—it's popular music, heath says; i like it, sometimes—are they listening? eyes focused on her, staring into the distance, or at the orchestra—

notes across a page, leaves across the sidewalk dried and blowing like natalia's hair as she walks against the wind, snow coming down, creating a blanket around her shoulders and hair; mittens, to keep the hands of a woman warm, america, waiting for a man in a uniform to write a letter to her, can you see when he'll come back? into the future, america looks, into a mirror, brushing her hair by the light of a lamp, cut flowers, a vase on a table, a quilt across the bed; pictures above the piano, red velvet seats, eyes of an audience focused, an opera glass that turns, under the stars, into the light of a room, shadows falling, fading under the moon, a man who looks at a woman walking away; a man with blue eyes and black hair, wiping with an apron his hands, a man who stands in the dark of a room, neon against a windowpane, streetlights reflected on the pavement, as natalia steps up an aisle wearing white shoes; but there is no stained glass, no one suspended on the wind, arms stretching to the sky; carry me across; behind a door, music playing, natalia looks through the window of a practice room, at a man playing on the percussion instruments; what was that? a thirteen chord, heath

says, but i can't write the rhythm out—a man on saxophone looking at natalia, as across the miles america looks, across the ocean
where a man wears a uniform, writing a letter to her as she waits, a
ring on a finger, sun glinting off gold, the ocean waves washing a
message to shore, clear as glass, music written for violin and flute,
clear and dark the water, the stream where a woman's dreams are
carried, to a man holding a hat in his hands; what is he waiting for?
    a man wearing an apron as natalia walks away and he watches
from the window, shared demise; drinking a bottle of coke, a vase
holding cut flowers over glass, walker says, i won't be gone long—
over the ocean connecting two lands, an island, a bridge that
natalia walks across, an echo as she steps, to see the light of day
streaming through a window, into the mist, natalia and heath walk
under an elevated train that clacks above them, span of gold wire,
across a river, beyond sounds that are flowing, under the bridge of
an instrument, beneath a window where someone walks, turn of
a clock, wheels sparking rails, orange against a black night, clouds
obscuring the stars, with no moon, above, sky like the still of a
river current, underneath an umbrella or a parasol on the beach,
walker as he walks away, wearing a uniform, carried across the sky,
across the continents, tides carrying sand to a beach where anastasia looks for america as she waits for a man, for a message that
falls to the ground, so that the old woman in the director's chair
takes off her glasses, to decipher the meaning of a note sitting on a
desktop, from a man who wears a uniform, counting the minutes
on a clock that spin by as the sun begins to disappear, behind the
clouds, into the ocean as though a beach ball over the waves, hovering before falling, the words of a man carried across a congregation
when walker comes home, taking america's hand, down a flight of
steps, a woman wearing crimson skirts and a black hat, who has
bobbed her hair, into a mirror she looks, into the glass, bending
the frames minutely, a fragment, just a little bit, walker as he wears
his glasses, sun reflecting off the lenses, like off a river or the waves
of an ocean, as he reads the lines natalia has written, celia looks up
from where she is sitting, piano notes flowing, slam of a door and

walker folds the letter, placing it on a desk beside a pen, no sound through the silence; natalia, combing her hair—

i won't wear a dress—; walk down an aisle wearing white shoes, carrying a bouquet of flowers in her arms; america, wearing trousers, walking through the woods, wearing a hat and fishing creel; staring into the mountains and trees, a woman who looks at a man; does he have something to say, something to tell her now; feet, sound of footsteps that echo against a trail on a night when no moonlight shines down; is she carrying a lamp, light carried to a city, across the waves, a man in uniform, waiting to come home; america asks, when will he come back—holding her head in her hands, tears streaking down her face; under the hand of a man, a child who is stirring in the dark—walker, america says, after anastasia, who went walking through the woods, disappearing into the trees, beneath the stars, a fire, ashes glowing, light that is turning, growing in the dark, a symphony, a woman singing in a practice room as the silence lifts like mist, stirring a discordant sound from instruments, from the feelings of a girl, her past carried with her, like the sound of ocean waves carried in a shell, sounds that rise and recede, chime of a triangle, notes on glass, fanny mendelssohn, praying, in the past; as snow begins to fall, nadine, putting a black coat on, tying her hair back against the wind that blows leaves across the sidewalk, into the air; hair falling against a face, light reflected against glass as nadine listens to music where someone improvises jazz tunes; a glass on a table, smoke that billows, particles in the light, hovering, notes carried to where natalia sits; erika says, cole porter, john coltrane—

i haven't heard this, heath says; where have you been—in the confines of a practice room—one day, the music of another time will have a part; one day, a woman will stand on stage, holding flowers in her arms as the audience walks away; a voice through the smoke, singing clear and hollow and long, notes from another time; bass chords, one instrument playing, sounds through the air, a plane under a night sky, turning in close to a river, buildings that rise to sway high above the earth, under the streetlights, traffic flowing, a mass of people, a window that is open, above the sidewalk in the rain, in a city where traffic stops and a taxi horn blows, yellow lights and green, black and white of a taxi cab, cacophony of voices, in a church, in the wings, steeple rising above stained glass, a grey building made of stone; st. thomas—, heath says; down an aisle wearing white shoes, turning to look at the glass—you don't have to believe in everything—, natalia says; above the silence of the church, what was the meaning—words, carried across a congregation, a chorus singing from church pews, putting their hands together to pray, in the silence under the church window, a pulpit where a bible rests, someone in a black robe, writing words to be carried down an aisle, in a black gown, someone who prays— what is he asking for, heath asks natalia—does he hope for something, someday—the thoughts of a girl, written across lines; creating a vi- sion in time, a man in an apron, as though in a dream; the eyes of someone staring, does he carry notes on wings or paper clips on piano strings, eyes with pinpoint focus, like stars reflected against the current; natalia pulls the line, the bubble that floats above water; she lifts the line, whipping it against the wind, floating it before she lifts it again, like the wind lifting the hair on her back, flying up before falling softly down, so that she cannot feel the imperceptible breeze that carries her to where she once stood beside a stream; does natalia wonder at the sight of a woman whose gaze falls upon her, the woman taking dark glasses from her eyes and holding them in her hand, two coke bottle glasses, impenetra- ble as the moon, filtering through the grass to the ground below, sand and rocks; nothing growing here, walker thinks, as he puts his fishing creel down—

the sound of a girl singing in an apartment, brass of a lock as she opens a door, opening the window blind to let the sun shine across the floor, on the piano where anastasia's picture sits, like a diary, sitting still on a desk, flowers on a table, water in a vase; a recording natalia plays, george crumb, notes written in circles, heath looks at the lines; i don't think i could ever read this—a processional, heath says, i've never listened to that—charles ives and bartók—folk and classical—ellen taaffe zwilich; i don't like it much—you're not used to it yet. it sounds as though someone could play any combi- nation of notes—as though you could play almost anything—and

i could be anyone, natalia thinks, i could be anywhere, writing
down notes—walking across a bridge, span of gold wire—but your
pieces are different—there has to be some kind of order, if the music conveys an emotion—one day, the sound of these instruments
will fade, gold into black, like flowers natalia picks, setting them
in a vase; purple and white, above the grass that is blowing, wind
stirring dust above a trail; mere particles in the wind? a chorus that
sings in white robes under bright lights, chime of a triangle, click
of fingers against a vase, wind from the open window blowing back
natalia's hair, as traffic sounds below, covering notes of the recording she listens to, before closing her eyes to see instruments flowing
above her, in a stream, a chorus of women, a curtain lifting, lights
shining on a man who dances in white tights, turning across the
stage, arms thrown out, was it only a dream—a tear that falls into a
puddle where a young girl looks, causing her reflection to shake minutely, a fragment, just a little bit; drapes blowing against the wind,
natalia closing her window as the sounds of the street fade, is it only
the percussive echoing of feet against a trail, wind rustling papers
across the floor, leaves across the sidewalk, brushing the sidewalk
like hair; silhouette, a shadow against the glass; it's already dark—
close the shutters, the light across the street—traffic flowing, taxi
horns, above the sound of rain falling; heath and natalia walk down
the sidewalk, through puddles they step as though down an aisle—

two percussive sounds, as heath unsnaps his violin case and
erika sings, rays of moonlight fragmented by street lamps where
natalia walks with heath, into a room where light reflects off gold
and brass, black and white of a piano, the percussion instruments;
there he is again, erika points to a table, the one who watches you—
what is his name? reid—erika, in a black dress and white shoes,
gold band around her neck, singing in the dark of a room; does reid
put his book down, as natalia walks out a door, into the fog that
lifts above streets, orange sparks against black tracks; erika, under
the lights of a stage, a piano playing while heath plays violin; leaves
across the sidewalk, dried and blowing, carried by the wind; notes
that fall above a river, into the water; the sight of a woman fading
as she looks into the night sky, does she begin to pray against the

time that will enfold her like wings; the woman in the director's chair who hears this melody, notes across a page, across a floor, scattered and blowing to where an audience sits, gold of an opera glass focused, a picture on a piano, anastasia, hair flowing out behind her, like the ribbon bound to her hat as she carries a walking stick, walking down a trail on a dark night, when no moonlight falls softly on her shoulders and hair; voices from a church pew, notes, created in the future, when a man stared out a window, looking down a trail; can you carry me across, dear reader, to a time not so fraught with memory—

above the piano, pictures of anastasia and america sit, carried beyond a clock that is spinning, natalia, standing by the rails, waiting for a train that will take her beyond the place of her childhood, mountains and trees, a river flowing beside tracks and natalia gazes out the window, sitting next to heath; a part in five-eight and one in four-four; heath says, i don't know how to put together these parts—light of a sign that is fading, into the dark behind a curtain, natalia closes her eyes; don't faint, heath says; i won't—that was a long time ago, natalia says, i've performed a lot of pieces since then—carried across an ocean current, a beach ball hovering over the waves as the sun starts to go down; walker looks at the old people below, sitting in the director's chairs; howdy, camper—howdy, stranger—the woman takes dark glasses from her eyes; natalia, taking a fish off the line, walker—a whisper carried through the leaves, rustling of branches as someone steps down a trail, ribbon tied around the brim of a hat that catches against the wind so that anastasia puts her hand on top of her head, to keep it from coming off. a hatpin, a pearl; a conversation, that voice; that surrounds us, even though the blackness cannot be seen, because the sun has not yet set, dear reader, above the trail.

how much further do we have to go? i don't know, nadine. natalia unlaces her hiking boots, and from one shakes out a stone, looking into the sky—

can you see this man dressed in white?

turning, in a field, anastasia leaning on her walking stick, grass blowing against the wind, houses and lights dotting the valley where anastasia lives; still point of a clock turning, america, waiting for a man to return, after a boy is born; america, carrying him in her arms down a trail, shadows falling under the sunset, in the dark, where america has grown; a ring on her finger in a picture that anastasia keeps; a man who once sat at a desk in the boarding school, in a uniform, traveling across the miles; america asks, when will he come back? a tear that falls on the floor beneath her feet, america, wearing a crimson dress with white lace; anastasia says, i don't think you should wait—for the message of a man; waiting to be born, a boy who will wear blue overalls, a railroad cap; tying his shoes, a woman who takes his hand, walking up the trail; america, putting a worm on a hook as walker pats the dirt with his hands; america—when will he come back? from a land that enfolds him, like wings; a hand that is held out, a ring on the hand of a woman in a picture, a woman whose gaze falls across a mirror, carried by the current of a breeze, like words of a man spoken to a congregation, still; carried like a night breeze rustling through silk robes of women who stand under bright lights, black night sky falling as natalia conducts a piece; someone who stares at the sight of a woman carrying a violin and notebook, walking into the silence that enfolds her, where he cannot see nor imagine the sound of taxi horns above traffic flowing, below streetlights where natalia walks up-hill and through glass doors; walking up a trail, america, putting a worm on her hook as walker watches, making designs with a stick in the sand, and america throws the line into the water, sitting beneath a tree—look—a fish that swims close in to shore, looking at america and walker, before it swims away; does it swim to the pond below, plants and rocks lining the water before the people come with the di-rector's chairs, before a girl takes a diary from a dresser drawer, dust on the cover, pages cut and fraying; a woman wearing a pink gown as her sister cut her hair, as into a looking glass she would look, tears streak-ing down the face of a girl whose father will not speak to her, after she cut her hair; words wafting up in the air and then falling down, as she walks down an aisle, a bouquet of flowers, a white dress, a pearl on the hat that she takes off before running her fingers through her hair; is he listening, do you think? do you think he understands, as he stares into the trees, mountains looming above him, beyond the trail where he stands, a woman has created these sounds against the black night, under a starry sky, a woman carrying a walking stick and wearing a pink gown, calling out a name—

america—you've torn your dress again—written in a diary, words read by a man, as natalia walks through glass doors, down the hall, looking through the window of a practice room; i don't think i'll ever do that, she says to heath, looking at anastasia's picture on the piano; i can't imagine that something would last forever—walking down an aisle wearing a white gown; flowers over a banister, petals across a stage—when will i find the time. it's six o'clock, heath says; wait—i'm coming with you—tears streaking a face; america says, i didn't know he would cry so much—more than you did, anastasia says, you were happier, as a girl—a man writing a letter from across the miles, until he comes home, to the town where he was born; writing in a classroom, anastasia, writing notes on the board; sitting at the dinner table, i didn't think he even noticed her, he never said a word—but he wrote notes, america says, that he put under my door; walking in the woods, a man holding the hand of america; picking flowers, in the folds of an apron, putting a worm on a hook; here is where we will sit, america says, as she puts the picnic basket down and she and walker sit, taking sandwiches from the basket and spreading a cloth beneath a tree; putting a worm on a hook, she throws it into the water, planting a stick to hold the line, until it pulls taut from the tug of a fish; america pulls the line with her hands; anastasia will clean it, america says, hitting the fish, hard on the head; and walker says, i didn't know you knew how to do that—

walking alone, up a trail on a starry night, someone worried and calling out her name; anastasia says, america went out with walker; does america's father sit down and sigh in the confines of a room; he is older than her—he's eighteen, anastasia says, and she's already sixteen—yes—she shouldn't go out with him, by herself. but he never says anything, anastasia says, i never thought he noticed her. until she cut her hair—bobbed hair and a black hat; she wears your clothes, whenever she goes walking now—they don't look good on her—but then, she would always ruin her dress—cut and fraying, across the lines—and i had to sew them, or buy a new one—robert shakes his head. at the opening of a door, the sound of footsteps up stairs; america, you've been gone too long—but the sun has barely set; i brought flowers from the meadow—she takes a fish from the picnic basket, and we can cook this for dinner—anastasia stands up from the table, i can clean it—and change your clothes, america—why don't you wear a dress. america sits down and unlaces her hiking boots; robert says, i don't think the two of you should go walking together, in the woods, alone. we went fishing, america says, we took a picnic basket—wearing a white dress with pink lace, a woman brushing out short hair and unlacing hiking boots; a thousand hooks and eyes, before lying on her bed, one hand on her forehead, her other arm at her side—

in the morning, before the sun comes up, america puts on her father's flannel shirt and khaki pants; anastasia says, you'll have to roll them up; and you should make sandwiches—anastasia says, i hope your father doesn't see you this morning—he'll see me when i get back—if he sees you now, he won't let you go—hiking with walker, and wearing his clothes—but you don't mind, america says—did she never tear the fabric, cut and fraying—i won't keep sewing your dresses up. and walker never says anything—anastasia wraps the sandwiches in paper before handing them to america; and a bottle of water to drink—america picks up the basket, letting the door shut quietly behind her, walking through the grass, hidden by the mist; wake up—it's already morning—not letting walker rest; he throws on pants and a jacket; then, where are we going? i'm not sure, america says; up the trail, where flowers are growing—she stops for a moment, to dig worms from the earth, putting them in a jar, why don't we go this way—as the sun starts to rise, over the trees; at the call of a robin, look—a fork in the trail and the mist disappears above the earth, evaporating under the sun; this is where we will sit, america says, as they approach a clearing and a pond, and america puts a worm on the line; gathering flowers in the meadow, until the sun begins to go down—we should be going, now, down the trail; or they will worry about us—she puts the fish in the picnic basket, and a hat on her head, staring at the sky above her, and the trees, as they walk down the trail, there's a candle in the window—, america says, opening the door and stepping across the floor; steps, up the stairs, as america walks inside, you've been gone a long time. can we put these in a vase?

staring into a night sky, into the abyss; a spotlight, a cone of light, falling on the sidewalk, rain; the clear sound of someone singing, a woman wiping with an apron her hands, raising her arms to the sky, as the sun begins to go down behind her, on the hills, sun rays slanting through trees and anastasia looks at the sand and rocks below; nothing growing here; glass of a cathedral window brightly stained above the piano where natalia plays, accompanied by an orchestra, notes, green disappearing into black, as the notes disappear, a woman in a white gown looks in a mirror, brushing out her hair; does she begin to understand that a man in the meadow never questioning her world will walk down a hillside carrying flowers or a girl—the notes that begin to flow from the point of a pen; hair falling across a face as a glance falls from the moon, in the silence of a room, dark glasses shielding a gaze that grows beneath the confines of a man's hand; one day, the silence will begin to fade, at the strike of a baton on a podium, a stream of notes, coming from within the silence, in the confines of a room; the curtains as they blow in the breeze, below sunlight that shines on the street, taxis and cars in a ribbon of traffic that flows beneath natalia's window, ribbons over a pair of dancing shoes, as the sun shines down between leaves, creating crooked patterns on the pavement below, cracks in the sidewalk as natalia walks across; as the past disappears behind, wheels turning across black tracks, tires against a runway, feet against a trail; natalia—

a voice calling in the distance, a whistle or the call of a bird, a sound from a long way off—a path that turns beneath wheels, over a dirt road as walker drives away from the ocean, into a meadow, a cabin on a trail; this is where we will live, robert says, laying wires across the land, like tracks of a railroad once laid down by a boy, wearing overalls, a blue hat, taking anastasia's hand as they walk more swiftly down the trail, dust disappearing above a dirt road, the glare from anastasia's straw hat, pink ribbon tied around the brim; a hatpin, a tear that falls, streaking a face, as the sun disappears beyond the ridge where anastasia looks for america, wearing black lace and bobbed hair, a crimson dress and a black hat, twisting the ring on her finger, a gold band; waiting, for the message of a man, at a time before walker is born, america, in a flannel shirt, tying a hook on the line, tying a knot, sitting beneath a tree; walker—when he comes back, wearing a uniform, america, walking down the aisle, flowers thrown over a banister, or onto a stage where a man speaks in a black robe, does someone begin to understand a man in the meadow never questioning her world; turning to walk down the aisle between church pews, tears streaking a face as water falls from the sky and into the stream, creating a splash; america—walking on the bank of a stream, away from the pulpit, the chime of a church bell; america—walking down an aisle in a white gown, into the arms of a man whose words enfold her, angels' wings, above the earth like mist, above a meadow, the sun begins to rise, creating a halo around natalia's hair, bright lights above women in white robes, sleeves billowing in the wind—

erika, in a black dress with dark skin and gold shoes, singing a melody, by a stream, america turns, at the sight of fish swimming, still, in the pond; she throws out her line, sitting beneath a tree, gold band around her finger, a letter from a man across the ocean, gold glinting off the water as the sun shines on a beach where a woman walks, a parasol shading her from the sun; candlelight reflecting against a windowpane, the reflection of a girl putting a hand against her face, staring out, into the night—what is she looking for? robert asks; walker, anastasia says; he's coming home tonight, we're meeting him at the train—eyes staring from behind the glass of a picture that hangs on the wall, as though suspended on the wind, leaves blowing across the tracks where america and anastasia shade their eyes against the dust that hovers, carried on the wind, sound of a train whistle wailing; words falling from the lips of a man, carried over the water, hovering on the waves, a girl who stood marking with her footprints the sand, the tracks of a bird; america—anastasia says, brushing her hair, in black waves down her back; anastasia, wearing a blue dress with white lace; candlelight reflecting against a windowpane; against the floor, fragments of moonlight through the window where anastasia cuts america's hair; the weight of a child that she carried; the boughs of pine trees that bend, as though they might begin to break at the current of the wind or snow that falls from the sky, onto sand and rocks below a mountaintop, where a cabin sits as though beside a beach, a white wood frame house, a cabin with shutters, black trim; strands of hair falling to the floor; a knock against the door as wind blows hard against the shutters, creating a sound, wheels against a track, screech of a train whistle, a man who steps toward america, standing beside the railroad tracks; the train as it pulls in and slows to a stop; america, walker says—

the bough of a pine tree that heaves in the wind, a sigh through the trees carried through the woods, across the mountains, the ocean current, across the waves, walker, wearing a uniform, staring into the eyes of america, wearing a ring he has sent her; america, covering her eyes as she imagines another time, a man as he steps, falling, leaves that begin to turn the gold colors of autumn, and america thinks to roll her trousers up, wading into the stream; lifting the line from the water, she pulls in a fish before putting another worm on the hook, sitting beneath a tree; leaves rising like dust, into the future where anastasia looks; teaching in the boarding school, pen across a page, does america begin drawing in school, pictures she creates, like words of a diary, in a desk, a gold key that anastasia wears on a chain around her neck, until the voice of a man carries the weight of his words, a gold ring around a finger heavy as the sound of rocks falling down a mountainside, into a pond; the woman, who moves the director's chairs around the shore; rocks tumbling, crashing into the pond below, creating a splash, water that falls as though from buckets on america, where she waits for a man to step down from the train holding a suitcase in his hand; walker, wearing a uniform, steps beside tracks, america as she runs, carrying in her arms a bundle of flowers; concave projection of an altar, voices in a church, in the wings, a woman walking down an aisle with black hair and a white gown, leaves in a whirlwind, falling onto the ground where america and walker stand, holding each other's hands; anastasia walks toward them, arms that enfold her beneath stained glass as a man speaks, dust hovering in the air where america walks with walker—

a locomotive gathering steam until it pulls away, taking america and walker to another point in time; a girl in a crimson dress wearing a gold ring, a diamond that is placed; a white house with black trim, candles in the window as america walks out the door, does she begin to think of a time in the future; a girl who rolled her pants above her knees to go wading into the stream, pulling the line in with her hands; hitting a fish, hard on the head, wearing a hat to shade her eyes from the sun, the dust, or sunlight glancing off her ring and into the eyes of a man, does he see a woman walking down an aisle, wearing black shoes and carrying orchids and roses to the accompaniment of an orchestra, a chorus of women in white robes who begin to sing, the melancholy accompaniment of a woman who once stood in a meadow, smoothing the folds of her skirt beneath her hands, her skirt flowing out as anastasia pins the fabric; to here— yes—hair falling to the floor in the path of moonlight that shines through the window where two candles sit; america says, i like it this way—and your dress—walking down an aisle, eyes focused on her as she walks with walker, up steps and through a door—

here is where you will sleep, anastasia says, smoothing the quilt on the bed—a patchwork quilt, a window looking out on the mountains and trees—a black suit and a red rose that walker pins to his lapel—orchids and roses—a gold band—anastasia says, turning under the hem of america's gown, where will you stay? traveling across the country; he could practice in a small town—; anastasia says, i know nothing about medicine—tears across the lines; until the clock chimes—click of heels against a wood floor, fingers tapping against a vase, ashes falling, wispy trail of smoke as anastasia walks, can america see beyond the stained glass window, into the churchyard where flowers stand; a wreath, over stone, the words that a white man speaks; what does he pray for, as america walks to the piano accompaniment; america and walker, beneath the pulpit, words hovering above them like notes carried by the wind, beyond the river current; america and walker, placing rings on their fingers, cast in stone; petals, floating in the air before falling beneath a banister, falling to a young girl's feet, a bouquet of flowers, fragments of moonlight floating beneath the window, where a young girl watches a young girl watching, and sitting on the grass, beneath a tree, throwing a line into the water, until she feels the line pull beneath her hand and she brings the fish into shore; the woman carrying a bouquet of flowers, a notebook and opera glasses in hand so that she can see in imagination, the gold of a woman's hair, or a bird flying beyond the ocean waves, the voices of women singing in a chorus in the church pew; america—

looking beyond the glass, anastasia asks robert, can you see her yet? holding walker's hand, america steps from a black car; walker, america says, your grandmother—walking in the woods, anastasia carrying a walking stick as walker builds castles in the sand by the side of a stream or lays down railroad tracks, sticks and weeds, blown by the wind when anastasia walks down the trail, at the sound of thunder not so far away, does walker put his head in his hands and begin to cry; anastasia lifts him up to carry him in her arms, down the trail to where walker and america sit, in the living room, piano notes flowing from the phonograph that plays, by the piano, and america plays out the notes when it stops—pictures above the piano; a woman taking a diary from her desk; sitting at the piano, natalia writes a melancholy accompaniment for violins, a woman's voice; natalia asks, can you sing this part? the notes are too high, erika says; but you can reach them, i think—natalia says, what do they think about this? as dust rises behind them, churning, beneath the wheels of a train, beneath the tires as they turn across a dirt road, dust rising into the air, walker looks at anastasia, waving before she turns to go inside, a house with shutters, black trim; the car pulls away and walker waves back; robert taking from his pocket a handkerchief that he waves in the air, dust particles glowing against the wind; where have they gone, walker asks, looking for the house, beyond the trees; natalia—nadine—he takes off his glasses, wiping them with a handkerchief before covering his eyes; in this mountain meadow, natalia says, nadine—in her apartment, she looks down at the street—america, taking off the long cumbersome skirt—i'm glad i don't have to wear that—standing by the window, walker pulls the curtains shut and turns out the lights—rain streaking the glass—

one day, the hand of a woman will hold the hand of a boy; a ring around a finger, a gold band; the sun that glints off the ocean, or off a ring in summertime, when sunlight shines down through the trees, a small town where america's husband works as a doctor, and america draws, charcoal, ashes, by the side of a fire, trails of smoke rising over the mountaintops where anastasia stands wearing a straw hat; as the sun shines through lace curtains, america opens her eyes—one day, the sight of a woman in the meadow will fade, like smoke above the engine of a locomotive, a train as it pulls away, over the tracks, disappearing, into the silence, so that it cannot be seen nor imagined by someone who stands far away; beyond the place that enfolds them, like wings, or the arms of someone, as though suspended on the wind, shatter of glass, misty glow in the rain and there you stand, gazing up at the light through a window that shines under the moon, sound of piano notes creating an accompaniment over the sound of traffic flowing, rain, falling to the pavement below, like leaves that anastasia walks across; carry me in your arms; into the distance, the notes of another time, the notes of a clock chime; curve of black wrought iron, sound of steps on a stair, the turning of a lock, opening a door, a girl, brown hair flowing down her back, smooth as a river current, notes on a phonograph, turning, natalia looks out the window, wearing black pants and a white shirt, does walker close his eyes to see, a woman as she wades into the stream, surfacing, notes on violin, a woman casting a line into a stream; does walker begin to understand the meaning, a bow across strings, a ribbon tying back hair, the clear gaze of a woman conducting an orchestra, or sitting in the director's chair, wearing a white cotton visor on her head; cacophony of voices until someone turns the sound into a melody, on the strings of a violin, a piano, notes sung by a chorus of women, the voice of a woman with dark skin; what does she hope for, walking down a street wearing white shoes and dark glasses that glare against the sun, the moon as it begins to fall against a night sky, shattering into glass, in the dark of a room, under a lamp, in the studio where natalia lives, as the notes play on a phonograph and natalia laces her shoes, black shoes and a white tie, a woman looking to the sky as though a man suspended on the air, falling on the wind, a chain of notes as she begins to sing, a sound carried as though on a river current, a woman who takes a man's hand, standing in a white gown beneath an altar, ashes fall from the sky, falling to the ground, dust, light rain; the clock chimes, steps on a stair; staring, two girls who look into a mirror until they begin to shake the snow from a tree, cutting and carrying it down the hillside beside a stream in winter; through the glass, a dream of a cool and tranquil time when a woman stood in a clearing in the woods, wearing a white gown, a parasol, walking down a street, straw hat in hand, green ribbon around the rim; a woman wearing a crimson coat with white trim in the clearing of a meadow, by the tracks of a railroad, a locomotive, steam; does walker step down to the platform now, holding america in his arms, as snow begins to fall like hair across a face, a woman who cut her hair, beneath a black hat in the frame of a picture that sits, still on natalia's dresser; the sound of notes through the silence as america waits, drawing pictures of the land, a sea bird in the air; silver on the table, a table cloth of lace, candles; america, waiting for walker to come back—

someone puts the book he is reading down, closing eyes as his sight begins to fail; down a trail, a tree that is carried; america stands the tree up before handing walker an ornament that he ties to a branch; a woman carrying a boy in her arms, beneath her skirts, to protect him from the light of day that will fall on him, at the moment he is born; the cry of a boy waiting for a man; anastasia, who lifts him up and carries him, into his mother's arms, as america thinks to name him; walker—after his grandmother, who went walking through the woods—did she never tear the fabric, cut and fraying, across the lines; a sigh in the breeze, anastasia, mere leaves above her in the wind that blows the ribbon behind her hair, her hair that once was so long, tangling in the breeze; sailing into a stream, a dream that carries her, down steps to the light of day; america, taking walker's hand when he comes back; lace curtains hang from a window, as walker picks up his bag and walks out the door, a black car, a dirt road that carries him to a house in the distance; a white frame house, black trim; a bed of roses; a ring on the hand of a woman in a white dress who looks across the waves, the woman who takes dark glasses from her eyes, lacing black boots and walking down a sidewalk as snow begins to fall, creating a blanket over her shoulders and hair; a quilt over a bed; a desk, a diary, pages cut and fraying, across the lines; does walker open his eyes, as america lifts him up and carries him, into anastasia's arms, as the road disappears behind them, through the meadow and trees; a house beside an ocean, boats; america, on the beach wearing no shoes, black hair and black pants, holding a fishing rod by a stream, brushing a picture with paint; mother, walker says, this is from anastasia—

america takes the telegram from his hand, shared demise—; does she begin to understand, a man in the meadow never questioning his world, laying wires across the land, wearing a ring on his finger, underneath stained glass, a black robe enfolding him like the words a man speaks, as america, anastasia, and rebecca stand, walker holding his father's hand as dust falls from the sky, a man's name cast in stone; robert, the weight of a man who carried his name, when anastasia gave birth to a girl, who once ran through the woods carrying a straw hat, wearing a long dress; the weight of a father's words who would not speak to her sister, when she cut her hair, when the length was so long, coiled in a mass; flowers thrown over a banister or onto a stage, into stone they are cast; anastasia, staring into the abyss as dust begins to fall like light rain over her shoulders and hair, the bough of a pine tree that bends under the weight of a breeze, snow as it begins to fall in the meadow and walker places an ornament on the tree, cut from the meadow where it once stood, blowing against the wind; anastasia, covering herself with a quilt, staring at the hat that hangs above her dresser; closing her eyes—dark night sky surrounding her, clear as a river current, as her sight begins to fail; clear and dark, the water, the stream where a young girl casts her line; america—when her words are spoken, a man who listens to a woman's voice, as though from a dream wafting over a mountaintop; when finally they are heard, a chorus of women's voices, walker turns to see the sight of a woman who walks away from him now, disappearing behind stage, flowers thrown over a banister, does natalia hold them in her arms; flowers, covering a man's name, cast in stone; anastasia when she turns in the field and is gone, ribbon flowing out behind her hat—dear reader, is she wearing one now? or has it been left behind, to the accompaniment of the stream, the man's words, no longer heard, the voice of a man who once stood beside her when she wore a white gown, as though in a dream, as the past slips behind her, as she walks down a trail to a house where no one stands; even if you look, you can no longer know her complications and turns, in a meadow, where she has gone; a house beside an ocean, a harbor, boats, a gold band around her finger as she writes the portrait of a man in the silence of her room—walker—a boy waiting for his father; he'll come back soon, america says; at the turning of a page, gaze into the glass, you will see another woman, walking by the stream as the sun begins to set; feet, the sound of feet hitting a trail, rain falling on the street where natalia walks, carrying a suitcase, like the weight of a man's words that will not be spoken; a tear that falls, clear and concise as the notes anastasia has written, above the abyss, falling, a night sky, an image of robert where he stood by the tracks of a train; anastasia and america, before walker comes back—

i don't think you should wait—for a man whose arms will enfold her, a gold ring around the finger of a woman who waits for a girl; walker when he is born, blue eyes open to the light of day; america takes his hand, walking on a beach, wearing a hat and running her toes through the sand; it is anastasia who picks him up to carry him, at the sound of thunder rumbling through the hills, when america cut her hair, and anastasia looked into the glass; not so distraught now, as the past disappears, underneath these wheels, carried smooth as a river current, to hawkes point, to north point, to a house and a woman holding a hat, wearing long skirts and still, america says, walking through the woods, where has she gone—

the road disappears behind them and anastasia waves, a handkerchief that she takes from her pocket, wiping the tears away; over a dirt trail, beyond the silence, before and after he is born, the tracks laid down by a boy on a hillside; anastasia taking walker's hand—does she begin to cry, at the sight of flowers that are sitting, still sitting—robert's name, cast in stone; the woman, holding a white cotton visor in her hand, beyond a point in time when a woman would wait for a man; in the silence of this mountain meadow, it is walker who looks at the tent, covered with rain; drops of water that have fallen to the ground below, covering the flowers and grass; natalia shakes the water from her boots, brushing out her hair, standing in the grass—it's cold, walker remarks—i'll warm my feet by the fire—nadine stirs the ashes until they are lit—don't drop the fish—nadine says, i won't—celia throws them above the fire, you should have come with us, nadine— next time, i'll go—i was reading this book—anastasia looks—what is that? natalia turns—a man in the meadow, never listening to her words—pages cut and fraying; i found them in her trunk—nadine hands the book to her; don't go dropping it, in the dirt—or above the fire—. natalia holds the book in her hands; the pages are crumbling— but her handwriting is clear—she taught writing, walker says, in the boarding school—your grandmother met your grandfather there— didn't he become a doctor, natalia asks; did they leave this place—a city with mountains and trees—across an ocean, a harbor, boats; as the past disappears behind, underneath these wheels; nadine says, she kept on teaching and writing after she was married; even after robert died— do you still keep that picture, nadine asks; above the piano—flowers, cut and fading—should we put these in a vase. natalia sits down, by the fire—it's hard to read, it's written so beautifully—that was just the way they wrote, walker says, everyone knew how to write back then— natalia asks, walker? did you ever read these—yes—locked up in a diary, had she thrown away the key—by the light of a lamp, natalia reads, before going to sleep; a woman who walked through the woods, lifting skirts over weeds, wearing a hat and carrying a walking stick, shading her eyes against the sun; closing her eyes to see: america—

when will she come back? fabric fading, like flowers sitting still, on a table, cut pieces of glass falling, broken from the moon, clear as a woman wearing a hat; in the clearing, at the sound of a whippoor-will, a time not so fraught with memory, even as the past appears in a mirror, as a woman brushes out her hair; but there is no ring on a finger, bobbed hair or black hats, no light colored lace; at the turn-ing of a page, natalia, wearing black pants and a white shirt, creat-ing sounds like lace, the rhythm of a straw hat that is swinging as someone runs, carrying it through the grass; overhead, the sound of a bird in the trees, the sigh of the wind as it comes down the hill, to where natalia and nadine sit, reading a diary by the brook, running their toes through the water; an image reflected in the pond where the woman and the old man sit, still sitting, solemn and quiet, fishing from the director's chairs as natalia and nadine walk closer to them; clear and dark, the water, the stream; can you see who stands in the clearing now, holding a hat in hand, wondering why has your sister cut her hair, as yours spills out from beneath the brim of your straw hat; a discordant sound, covering the silence like a blanket of snow, wafting over a mountaintop as though in a dream—natalia—nadine—does walker put his hands together; the clock chimes as natalia, heath and erika walk across black pavement; turning down a winding street, through a door, a man on saxophone, a man playing piano and a woman who sings in the dark night of a room, miles davis, nina simone; particles of dust in the air, light shining against the mist where it falls, obscuring light from the street lamps so that nadine cannot see natalia now, as erika begins to sing; a dream wafting, words spoken into the air by a man in a black robe who raises his arms to the sky; petals thrown over an ocean, an image of anastasia, floating, mere particles in the wind; fallen fragments of moonlight falling, is anyone there, nadine asks, as natalia looks into the sky where the image of a man is broken; dust flies up in the air, paper, gusting into the air and falling across the sidewalk, carried like steps on the wind, words flowing as though pulled by a river current—a man who carries a bouquet of flowers, cast in stone before he turns—a woman gazing at the abyss before she begins to discover a meaning, string or twine, wrapped around the finger of a boy or girl, lace on the dress that anastasia wears, in a picture, in a frame; words across the page of a diary that natalia reads, sitting by the fire—smoke, billowing from the fire like the dress that anastasia wears when she appears, glowing above the coals—the stars—the dipper—the coiled wood of a violin that natalia plays; at the opening of a door, a woman in a long gown who looks into a mirror, into the silence, hovering over the waves as the sun begins to set, above the current, the tides as they recede; washed to shore, surfacing, a long flowing gown; a man who looks, is she lost? under a starry night, the full moon above; someone worried and wondering, a man who looks into the distance, calling out her name—america—

in a field, carrying a hat; clear and dark, the running of a woman who looks at the hills that surround her, a night sky where someone bows her head; is she waiting for arms that will enfold her, in a dream; a man who appears, it is walker who looks for anastasia, underneath a straw hat, in a picture that is fading, beneath a stone that bears her name; where has she gone? someone who stares at natalia as she is walking away, under the light of the moon, clear as a ribbon that is fraying; carry me to the point in time where a man is waiting, standing in the fray, does he wear a jacket as he stares into the wind that runs like fingers through his hair, under a starry night where no woman can be seen, down a sidewalk, over a cup of coffee natalia says to heath, someone appears in my dreams—a percussive echoing; is there no one now to hold the hand of a boy as he closes his eyes, underwater, in the stream of fish flowing by; if he would reach out his hand, turn and walk to the bank of the stream where a message lies waiting for him as though written in the sand, by a woman wearing glasses to shield her eyes from the sun, as she sits in the director's chair and the sun begins to go down—behind the mountaintops, a woman carrying a lantern, no fishing rod in hand, three flowers that she has picked and put in her hat as she lies down to dream, water running over her face and into the grass, creating a stream that courses down the mountaintop like tears against a face; she pulls from her pocket a handkerchief to wipe her eyes, to see the pale vision of a woman, a bouquet of flowers thrown onto stage, where a man stands before turning to walk into the fog that obscures natalia's vision, so that she cannot see him, where the sounds of an orchestra carry him like music carried by the wind, as he fills a book with letters, writing with a feather pen; anastasia—does she say that a man came to the meadow; did a wind come to carry her across the green fields, where flowers blow in the current of the breeze; a woman whose gaze turns to the running of a stream, america looks at her reflection; casting their lines into the stream, she and walker sit, walker wearing overalls, a stick in his hand, writing notes in the mud—

natalia, walking down a trail on a dark night holding a lantern to light her way, to where nadine and celia sit, building a fire; but she cannot see them, and through the thick sound of branches blowing comes the song of a nightingale; or is it walker calling, nadine—but there is no voice of a girl in the room where natalia closes her eyes to sleep; anastasia—america says; sometimes she would wait until morning to come home, the first light of dawn reflecting against the windowpane, spreading across the floor as anastasia lifted the blinds and america sat, reading or sleeping, hair across her face, a red velvet seat, in the house that stands in a clearing, a small town, a boarding school beneath the hills where she goes walking every day, the weight of a ring on her finger reflecting the sunlight as she undresses to bathe; a child that is growing—does she begin to understand, a man who speaks to her, are you lost, from the clearing, where the sun no longer shines from behind the clouds, at the sound of thunder, rain, a bolt of lightning that strikes, splitting a tree, causing it to sway, and creak—like the opening of a door, natalia thinks, when she first hears the sound of his name—

the humming of wires that send a telegraph, a table holding a vase of white flowers standing still in water, a stream of tears that flow, under the light of a street lamp, the vision of a man begins to fade as heath carries his violin down the sidewalk and into his apartment where he practices, street noises covering the notes on violin, bow across strings, does heath begin to dream—a woman carrying a straw hat or someone who stands fishing beneath a tree in a long dress, standing by a stream of raindrops streaking down a windowpane; heath closes the curtains; closing his eyes to sleep, a sidewalk that falls into the ocean; i didn't hear you calling, natalia says as heath stands on the sidewalk; i was dreaming of someone—she lets him in the door and heath says, we should be leaving—natalia stands in the shower, water forming a puddle beneath her feet, the reflection of a teardrop, a pearl at the bottom of the pool as anastasia bathes, wrapping her hair on top of her head, brushing out the strands as she lies on a rock, running her hands through the grass, the flowers, as though they will not fade, like notes of a phonograph or a picture that is taken, click of a shutter, fastening of a latch, as anastasia sits in the sun and a man draws america; putting his work into a frame house, that will be walker, one day—

across a wood floor, creating the tracks for a train that brings
america to him, a castle with turrets, a moat, a door—a tear that
falls by the side of the fire after nadine is no longer sitting, still
sitting, is the woman in the director's chair someone we can, if we
shade our eyes against the setting sun, see in the distance, as natalia dries her eyes; no letter from a man; ring against a finger, tears
against a face; you couldn't go back, heath says, to live with dan;
under the sound that comes stirring, has the past so far faded that
no pictures or letters remain; only the sound of a distant echo, the
surf of the ocean that resounds in a shell that anastasia finds, by
the water where she and robert walk along the shore, on planks
of wood laid down by a man who ran through the woods wearing
overalls, flannel pants, a suit jacket, a hat, peach ribbon around the
brim as he stands, hands on his hips and wearing waders by the
side of a stream, where america and walker sit, a white cotton visor
shading her eyes from the sun that shines brightly on the people
walking below, down the trail—natalia—nadine—they can't hear
you now, walker says, as he holds america in his arms and natalia,
walker and nadine disappear from view, obscured by the trees; only
the sound of a whippoorwill above the fading echo of footsteps,
until there is no sound at all—

or is it the soft whir of a motor as walker starts his car to drive
on a dirt road to celia's house in the middle of may; a white car, a
dirt road, a house with shutters, black trim; or walker leaves a note
in the mailbox at the foot of the curving drive, sloping sharply to
the house below the hill, in a clearing by the stream; celia sits reading and waiting for him, on the porch of her grandmother's house,
listening for the motor of his car, dust rising in a cloud above the
dirt road, a white house; a bed of roses, a mailbox; no letter from a
man; across a room, reid watches natalia walking away, beyond the
flowers growing, to a place where there is a point of light, candle
light framing a window where a young man looks, glasses impenetrable as the moon when the sun shines through natalia's shades;
sitting still, beneath the window, cast in bronze, the statue of a militiaman, click of hooves against the pavement; or is it a young girl
in the confines of a room, in summertime, when moonlight shines

through a window—america—where has she gone—light a candle in the window for her.

can you see walker, as it begins to rain, on a street where celia waits, under the clouds that are hovering, as though in a dream, a man carries a letter to her where she waits, a window framed with lace curtains, dreams written beneath stained glass that shatters beneath a distant gaze; an accompaniment, flowing like the curtains blowing in an open window; a bed of roses, a house with white trim where celia carries a piece of wood held in her hand, a small bird, an egg, the voice of a woman who hasn't begun speaking yet; a pattern of shadows, falling where a woman sings, crying out to be heard, the voice of a woman whose words are written in a letter; charred and fraying, across the ocean, ashes thrown from a vase of flowers sitting, still sitting, collecting particles of dust like leaves, carried on the wind, a woman waiting for the words of a man to be spoken; under a bridge and through a door, can you see through the glass to another place in time, carried like a grain of sand in the palm of a woman; a pearl, a hatpin; a hat placed on the head of a woman, tied with ribbon around the brim, as she holds the hand of a boy, and begins walking down a trail before the sun has set—under an awning, under the moon, the words of a man that have not been spoken yet, across a page, anastasia puts the book she is writing in down—walker—she shades her eyes against the setting sun to see a man holding flowers, placed in the hands of a woman, before she looks into the bright lights that shine below, as though she is standing on stage; america, carried across an ocean current; drops of water falling down a window as america dries her hands and face, and anastasia leans against a tree, gazing into the future and thinking about the past, walker dries the tears from his eyes before tying a fly and wading into the stream, carrying two bottles of salmon eggs; the song of a bird that sings from a tree as walker bathes his feet in the stream; getting up to look, it is america, sitting up in bed, walking across a wood floor and raising the blinds, to see the fields where she walks in summertime, blades of grass bending beneath her feet as she walks beside the water, sitting beneath a tree and placing a worm on her hook that she casts into the pond, a ripple that causes her reflection to shake minutely, a fragment, just a little bit—

a ring around a finger, string or twine, a bow, tied around heath's neck like the ribbon that anastasia wears on her hat before unpinning america's dress, after sewing up the seams—a woman who raises her hands to the sky; is she beginning to hope for someone whose arms will enfold her, for the man carrying an envelope, words written in the sand or on a subway train, a man who looks like someone she has seen, in her future; leaves across the sidewalk, carried across a stream where a man is bathing in the middle of may, before putting on a flannel shirt and trousers—that will be walker, one day—a man will carry the dreams of a woman folded in his arms like a bundle of flowers, placed by the side of a stream before a woman can turn to look, does walker follow her gaze; under the sunlight, are the consequences of the moon beginning to pave the atmosphere an inconsequential gray, drawing the tides into a room where a woman paints the portrait of america in shades of gray, pouring down the aisles, cascades of a curtain as a ribbon begins to fray where the pictures of two women sit, under the white lace curtains that blow from the breeze carried across the ocean, the white foam of ocean waves carrying sand to this beach where a woman walks; america, wearing perfume, bobbed hair and a black hat, when a man carries her away, down an aisle; walker, before he is born, carried beneath the hand of a woman; when he finally appears, america says, walker—after you were gone—anastasia, walking through the woods carrying bright flowers and singing, wearing a hat as she carries walker in her arms, until they come to the end of the trail, a house in the woods, where candles have been lighted in the window for them—america says, you have been gone a long time—america, wondering about anastasia as walker looks into the distance, carrying a lantern and calling out her name—anastasia—celia turns to walk inside from the porch where she has been sitting; she turns the ring on her finger; wearing a ring that shines silver, connecting the tides to the moon, between heaven and earth, a man suspended on the wind, bearing alms that he hands to natalia, on stage before she disappears behind the curtain, under the stars as natalia walks down a street, fallen fragments of moonlight falling, tearing, a white gown sewn in the confines of a room as a young man waits; one day, a woman will walk down an aisle wearing a white gown, holding a bouquet of flowers in her arms and waiting for someone to pray—but there is no gaze from above; no one who quakes at the sight of grass as it chafes roughly against her knees; only a woman in the meadow who turns at the sound of notes playing, does she begin writing with a feather pen; one day, a woman will wear black to walk down an aisle, beyond the man who stands in a black robe, arms stretched to the sky, to the pulpit beyond; will she stand at the podium conducting an orchestra; shatter of stained glass beneath the steeple that rises, red carpet that sinks beneath her feet as she walks, a man wearing glasses, blue eyes and black hair, across the street, across the tracks of a subway train, a man who carries the weight of a woman as though in his palm, a man wearing flannel trousers, a straw hat with peach ribbon turned around the brim, standing in a field beside a dirt road, the church where he is to be married—

dust stirs beneath the wheels and walker drives down a winding road through the hills, a house with shutters, black trim; as the door slams does walker lean against the gate post, before he and celia walk down the sidewalk and through a door, drinking a bottle of coke, shared demise—america, walking up a dirt trail carrying a fishing rod and creel, over her shoulder, a walking stick in hand, wearing white trousers and a flannel shirt, her hat brim shields her face from the sun; did she tuck her hair up under her cap? the sound of a voice when it is heard, carried across the white foam of the ocean waves, in a street car, that will be walker's granddaughter, one day; a woman will walk down an aisle wearing a black suit and a silver ring, connecting the tides to this moon that shines, rays penetrating through the branches of trees standing high overhead, above the waters of this beach; practicing in the confines of a room, a woman with dark skin, is she lost—carrying notes of a distant harmony as though across the wind, her voice on a dark night, moonlight falling, dust in the air as the wheels turn and walker drives away; celia takes out a handkerchief to wave, before walking through the gate to her house, she opens the door, lies down on her bed and closes the blinds, closing her eyes to sleep, a hand over her forehead and one at her side—

america—sitting up in bed, at the sound of a robin's call; she walks across the wood floor, shakes out her hair and washes her hands and face, in a basin, drops of water falling by the light of a lamp; she picks a pair of trousers and puts on waders; kissing walker good-bye, across the wood floor, out the door and up the trail that is still lighted by the moon as she picks up a worm from the dirt and folds it on a hook—anastasia lifts walker in her arms, as he begins to cry—america's husband sits up in bed; walker—anastasia says, as he rubs his eyes—america went fishing—a woman who walks down an aisle wearing a white gown as though a man appears in her dreams; it is natalia who creates a melody to accompany anastasia, wearing a white hat and holding walker's hand, the melancholy sound of her voice when it is written; america, sitting up in bed—pulling on trousers, a white shirt, a hat to shade her from the sun, as walker opens his eyes to the light of day, she is gone—folding a worm on a hook, beneath a tree, waiting, until the sun begins to go down and anastasia comes looking for her, carrying walker in her arms—america—robert says to walker, look— as anastasia and america walk across the fields and back to the house, they've been gone a long time—

a grain of sand in a woman's hand, a hatpin, a pearl, a boy, a bundle of flowers in natalia's arms as she walks down an aisle wearing white shoes, across a bridge, span of gold wires, notes across the wires, a man suspended on the wind, gazing into the sky; walker, listening to the wind through the trees, a robin singing overhead as anastasia takes pins from her hair, and america walks down a trail, as though down an aisle where celia waits for walker; does she write a message in the sand by the side of the stream; wheels churn dust into the air, particles of dust glowing against the sun and celia shades her eyes, sweeping out the tent before folding it up to carry it down the trail, holding the hand of a girl—nadine—walking down the street as a foghorn sounds; natalia looks at the harbor, boats; a flagstone walk, the steps of a militiaman—or is it walker coming to the door where celia waits, holding an envelope in her hand; under the sky, a sound that comes tearing—america—pulling a dress apart at the seams; i can't walk in this—wearing a white gown and carrying flowers, a hat with white lace and bobbed hair—walker drives in a black car to a house in the clearing, up steps wearing flannel pants, carrying a bouquet of flowers, a letter thrown onto stage, the words of a man who is still, waiting, standing still and waiting for her—

natalia looks across the bright lights, across the tracks of a train does a dancer stand wearing white shoes, is he lost? under the sounds of the city; but it is only heath calling from the sidewalk, waking natalia—you were dreaming—a man wearing a ring on his finger, heavy as a weight of lead—i won't be gone long, walker says—does he hold celia in his arms; across the sky the sound of thunder tearing—a young girl crying in the meadow, rain against a windowpane; walker, in a uniform, waiting to come back across the continents, across the waves; stirring, under a night sky, a voice when it is heard; natalia—celia says, turning the ring on her finger that walker gives her before he goes away—under a starry sky, the full moon above, the tides wash a woman onto a beach, clear as a river current or a woman sitting and wearing a hat, and walker turns by the tracks of a train; anastasia sits on a rock under the bright sunlight; she finishes writing a letter and signs her name— at the sound of thunder, then rain, she and walker begin walking down the trail, does she hold his hand; a grain of sand, click of fingers against a vase; you were gone too long, robert says—or does he only turn his gaze away from the place in the meadow where a woman stands alone—against the sunlight that enfolds her, does she put her hands against her face, to see the vision of a woman who appears wearing a long dress—nadine? natalia stands by the fire, have you finished reading those yet?

reid takes off his glasses and rubs his hands against his eyes, then looks at natalia; celia looks in the glass; and natalia cups her hands, holding water from the stream, she washes her face; taking a handkerchief from nadine, cold and dark the water—walker takes off his waders; fragments of coals glowing, sparked before they are lit; we need more wood—nadine says, i went to get some—at the turning of a page, a hand that holds a hat as lightning strikes and rain begins to fall—take these inside, natalia—nadine hands her anastasia's diaries; how many have you finished reading? i've read almost all of them—had she locked them in a cedar chest, and thrown away the key; natalia looks into the sky at the stars above; a woman whose sight is fading; is this the woman, one and the same as the woman sitting in the director's chair; behind dark glasses, behind a veil that serves to shield her from a cascade of raindrops streaking down a windowpane at night, impenetrable as the moon, where america sits, tying a fly, as the sun begins to go down and walker calls, natalia—nadine—but there is no response; or is it only a woman wearing a white dress and holding flowers in her arms; cut pieces of glass fallen, broken from the moon; walker sits with celia, an arm around her shoulders as the sun begins to go down and they sit on the steps of her grandmother's house; the church steeple in the distance; but celia cannot see nor imagine who might be there, below the cross, a man in a black robe who folds his hands to pray; is he waiting for something to appear to him; a girl, wearing a cap and fishing dress, black pants and a white bow tie, walking down an aisle to no accompaniment, raising arms to the sky as the instruments begin to play, the man in the black robe; what did he say? that one day, a woman's life will disappear in the mist; at the turning of a page, reid looks at natalia as nadine binds anastasia's diaries with ribbon, you can keep these—; had someone thrown away the key—

mittens to keep the hands of a woman warm until walker steps down from a train in a uniform, holding america in his arms, across a dirt road, across the continent to a house by a beach, dust colored bedspreads and a parrot in a cage that sings; in a city by the ocean, away from the mountains and trees, a boy wearing overalls, clapping his hands and patting sand into a castle, sticks and weeds; or is it only the falling of a branch, the gold of an opera glass, or america as she listens to walker's words, at the tolling of a church bell, flowers thrown over a banister, under an umbrella on a beach by the waves, a clear bottle, glass reflecting against the sun—

beyond the waves, on the porch of a cabin, celia laces her shoes, meeting walker at a turn in the stream where they will bathe; celia holds a letter in her hand, sitting on the porch, beneath the moon;

casting a line into the stream, walker ties a fly as america plants her feet in the sand, a fish that pulls at her line; walker looks into the stream, a moment in time, blowing with the current of the wind, flowers that celia's mother picks, putting them in a vase, as though time will not fade an array of flowers beside the church pew; this is where we will live, walker says, staring across the field at the mountains in the distance; the slam of a door in the breeze—celia, down the porch steps to the road where walker waits, wearing a cotton dress that her mother has made, like a gown natalia sees, as a girl, running down a dirt trail as walker holds out his hand; walker—nadine says, and she and natalia walk down the trail to catch up with him, holding a picnic basket; on america's arm, a bunch of flowers, scattered to the wind, falling through the air as celia and walker drive away from the church on a dirt road, away from the mountains and trees, where anastasia walked as a girl—a bed of roses, a frame house—anastasia waves as the car drives away from the church; a man in a black robe who speaks to walker and celia, walking down the aisle, someone lighting candles at an altar—does he begin to pray—walker looks on the trail for celia and nadine; where have they gone? america shades her eyes to see—a man who comes looking for her as the sun begins going down behind the mountaintop; under a moon, the leaves begin to rustle in the breeze and walker stirs the coals of the fire, until they are lit, bursting back into flame—

a small house, white with black trim, where curtains blow in the breeze—walker drives down a dirt road to another town, white columns of a building, steps against a marble floor; anastasia holds his hand, and walker thinks what to say; they drive away on a dirt road, and america takes out a handkerchief to wave—not so far away, thinks walker, and he walks through the gate, up steps and across a wood floor, steps, dust colored bedspreads, on its perch in a cage, a parrot; walker hangs the cage from the ceiling; nadine, reading anastasia's diary by the light of a lamp; what did she say? that one day, a woman will turn in the meadow, at the tolling of a church bell, a clock that chimes, as walker walks down the stairs to class; a staircase that curves, where america throws flowers over the banister before she and walker drive away, on a dirt road, a car decorated with ribbons and bows; pink and purple, an array of white—

cast in stone, anastasia's name, when walker comes home in the spring, where has she gone? across the meadows and fields, the sound of a locomotive wailing, steam from a tea kettle where america sits, holding walker in her arms; at the chime of a clock on the mantelpiece, walker, walker and america, driving down the dirt road to the house where anastasia taught and walker went to school—shared demise—did a wind come to carry her, across the meadow where a man worked, laying wires across the land—until the sound of thunder, rain, dust blowing across a meadow, into a stream—

at the turning of a page, walker returns to school in the middle of may; carrying a straw hat and a walking stick, a box of books and letters, a picture of anastasia that he sets on his desk, a woman who looks in the light by a mirror; across the meadows, america, anastasia says—she must be sitting beneath a tree—pulling the line in her hands, as anastasia picks walker up to carry him in her arms, we will go looking for her—they come to a fork in the trail, where america and walker sit; sitting, still, the people fishing from the director's chairs as the sun begins to set behind the hills; walker looks at his mother; the people sitting in the director's chairs; what do they patiently await, dear reader, as walker and america stand by the side of the stream and america says, i didn't hear your step on the trail; anastasia leans on her walking stick, watching walker wade in the stream; america—her husband says, as a fish tugs on the line—and their son walker pulls on the line with his hands, the way that his mother has taught him to do; he throws the fish on the bank and america pulls out the hook; watching america hit the fish on the head causes walker to stare up at the sky; an opera glass that turns; the woman in the director's chair; that's enough for a meal, america says—we should be going back down the trail—; to the house where robert waits on the porch, like celia, on the steps of her house; walker plays by the side of the trail, running to catch up with america, walker and anastasia, walker, holding anastasia's hand until they arrive; a house with shutters, a man who looks, as anastasia and america walk inside—

across the lines, a picture that walker keeps on his desk at school, after he has moved away; in the white of a church where celia sits, under the stained glass, steps on a stair and there walker stands, where there once stood only the statue of a militiaman, his horse faltering in the wind; in the middle of may, carrying a picnic basket, walker and celia, spreading a blanket beneath a tree, as the minister takes from the basket chicken and eggs; walker, celia says, and the minister begins to pray; walker looks at his watch and celia says, my mother always went to church—staring into the distance, the minister looks away—she sang in the choir, says celia; and she played violin—; my mother, walker says, could pick out songs from the phonograph, she played them by ear—the clock chimes, and walker says, what did he say? he takes celia's hand and they begin walking downhill; i teach, celia says, in that school—natalia points down the hill, see the tent in the meadow, through the flowers and trees? yes—

nadine says, we don't have much further to go—at the sound of a whippoorwill singing above the trail walker takes off his hat and looks below, that's where i'm going to school; can you see through the trees? celia's mother shades her eyes against the sun; at the sound of a car engine, dust flies into the air; walker, celia says, to the mountains and hills beyond; walker stands on the porch at celia's house, or they sit at a cafe, drinking a bottle of coke, shared demise—

across a table, a vase full of cut flowers in the apartment where natalia works—a man who sees her, does he close his book as she walks down the street; drinking a bottle of coke, shared demise; walker places a ring on celia's finger in the middle of may, i won't be gone long—on the porch of celia's house, walking down the path to the stream where they bathe; walker, taking celia's hand, sitting in the church and celia says, i don't believe in what he has to say—that a man in the meadow never questioning his world will carry a girl, or a boy in his arms, string or twine, and sigh at a wreath of flowers placed over stone; that a woman who once went running through the woods will not disappear into the abyss; a man on a horse staring into the distance, cast in stone; walker and celia rise from the church pew, staring into the stained glass, natalia walks down an aisle and the orchestra tunes their instruments, as the performance is about to begin; walker wearing a uniform as he walks away; teaching in a small town, celia, after she finishes school, books across desks, typewriters, click of fingers against a vase; walker walks up the stairs to the school building, or celia and walker drive to her house, sharing a book or talking by candlelight, walking down a path, under a canopy or under the moon, driving to the house where walker was born, where america lives alone, after her husband has gone; did he disappear into the abyss; did a wind come to carry him, across the meadow where celia and walker drive, across a dirt road, to a white house with black trim, a bed of roses; america, as dust flies into the air, wheels churning, particles under the sun, after walker has gone, this is where you will stay—

america smoothes the quilt on the bed; walker and celia, walking to where walker's father lies now, his name cast in stone; walker—celia reads, and thinks, that will be his son, one day—a wreath that is placed before walker and celia return, down the path and on the dirt road that leads to america's house, does walker begin to cry, at the thought of a clock that is spinning above him, flowers fading and falling away; celia wipes his eyes with a handkerchief; the woman who turns around to stare, fishing, still fishing from the director's chair; a name cast in stone; a man who once went walking with america, rolling his trousers up to wade in the stream where america caught a fish, pulling at the line with his hands, throwing the fish up on the bank; america hits the fish on the head before putting it in their basket; walker—it's time to go home.

does the woman stand from the director's chair, pulling it closer to the pond, away from the sun; into the clouds, mist, as natalia walks down a street, a man on the corner, drinking a bottle of coke, shared demise; natalia sits on a bench, reading a book; reid asks, what is that? my great-grandmother's diary, natalia says; america— he reads from the page; my grandmother's name was america—that was just how they named people, natalia says, everyone had strange names then—anastasia, reid says; she named her daughter america; anastasia taught in a boarding school, natalia says, she kept teaching after she was married—after her husband died—; my grandfather went to the boarding school, he met my grandmother there—; bobbed hair and a dress with black lace; above the piano, eyes focused on them; notes from the clock chime; natalia sees heath on the sidewalk and picks up her books, i'm late again—she runs to catch up to heath and erika, who is that man? he works in the cafe, natalia says, where we stop before class. i didn't recognize him on the street—wearing glasses and black hair; heath asks, is he interested in you? he's interested in my family—look. heath picks up the diary, anastasia—setting flowers in a vase; natalia's mother looks up at the sky; what should we play—clara schumann—; they walk through the building and the clock chimes, i wish we didn't have class—as the clock spins on the far side of the room, erika hums a piece, under the pulpit, under the moon, a ring placed on celia's finger, under the canopy where she and walker sit, i won't be gone long—in a uniform, across the ocean, as celia waits, shading her eyes to see—

america, standing by her house, waiting for celia and walker, after her husband has gone; celia and walker step down from the car; one day, walker says, we will live far away—in a mountain meadow, sitting by a pond or a stream, fishing, a man in the meadow never questioning his world; the sun starts to go down, and america, walker and their son, walker, walk down the trail toward a cabin in the woods; walker stands in front of america's house, holding celia's hand, a ring that is placed; at night, stars shine down on anastasia, sleeping as though on a rock in the meadow, until america comes through the door to find anastasia sleeping, still sleeping; sending a telegram to walker where he lives, working during the day and in school at night, arriving at the school where celia teaches, walking down the sidewalk; walker drives away to the town where he was born, anastasia turns and is gone; a trunk full of letters, and pictures in a case that walker gives to celia, to keep while he goes away, wearing a uniform, across the ocean, across two continents; diaries tied with ribbon—

stirring the coals of the fire, until it is lit, natalia asks, what did you say? i'm going back to school, nadine says, to study medicine—but that will take forever. i'll be finished by the time i'm thirty—walker asks, are you sure that's what you want to do? i always liked being in school, and i'm tired of working in the bookstore—and i barely make enough money to pay my rent. at least you, she looks at natalia, do something that you like—walker says, people like your mother and i—celia—add some wood to the fire—it's getting cold, natalia remarks. i'm going to perform another piece—and then what will you write? i haven't decided yet—the trees sway in the wind; what was that? celia asks. just a falling branch—

celia, natalia, walker, and nadine sit, after the sun has set; can you see them? natalia asks. the people in the director's chairs. anastasia, writing her thoughts, the woman in the practice room, or in the director's chair; the song of a girl, singing, as her father stood on the trail, fishing in the stream; howdy, camper—howdy, stranger—i didn't catch any fish. sitting—writing notes—walking down an aisle, wearing white shoes—are you ready? yes—

so you finally met someone? rebecca asks. a man came to town; an electrician, anastasia says. laying wires across the land—anastasia picks up the dress she is sewing; her mother says, but you will be living far away—across the mountains and oceans—we may spend time in another town—; rebecca asks, then you won't keep teaching school. anastasia's mother takes the kettle from the stove, where will you find the time? you won't have children? at least, not right away—the sound of a stream that is flowing; anastasia's mother says, it's too hot outside—i think we should go bathe. anastasia, rebecca and their mother walk down the path through the woods and undress by the pond; anastasia's hair tangling around her head, or coiled in a mass—i want to do something, besides staying home all day long. but i stayed home, her mother says; why would you rather be gone? until i have children—and even then, robert can help take care of them. rebecca closes her eyes. at least both of you are getting married—you should have someone to share your life—anastasia turns to their mother, robert likes to go fishing, and he doesn't mind if i go alone—have you finished drying off? my hair is still wet—it's nice to have someone to talk to—i still miss your father—anastasia's mother buttons her dress. but he wouldn't speak to me, rebecca says, after i cut my hair—that was a long time ago. walking down the trail to the cabin—why don't we sit outside—

we have to fold up the tent—and make sure you shake off the water—it's too heavy to carry, if it's wet. will it fit in your pack? yes, says
nadine. in the morning as the sun is coming up; will we have time
to fish? nadine asks; then, natalia can keep working on her piece—

walker says, there is a place where we can stop on the trail, nadine—you will have to put waders on. why did she write so much?
she just liked writing, walker says; everyone liked to write back
then. it's interesting, natalia says, just reading how she thought—
nadine lifts up her pack, can you carry this? natalia puts anastasia's
diaries in a pouch. have you read all of these? i finished them—and
the letters in the case. where is this place on the trail?

the notes of a clock chime; natalia puts her notebook on a desk;
in the confines of a diary, had she thrown away the key—how much
further do we have to go? we're almost there, walker says—and we
can fish here, in this pond. nadine takes off her pack, you don't want
to use the fishing rod? no; and you can put my waders on. nadine
wades out to the middle; then, i've got a fish. how big is it. natalia
looks up from her notebook, give it some slack—walker wades out;
i can reel it in—i've got it—nadine holds it in her hand. why don't
we just eat vegetables, natalia asks. but walker says, we won't keep
any more. lacing up her hiking boots, natalia says, i didn't think
you knew how to do that—but i went fishing with walker, while
you were gone. and you don't mind cleaning them now—walker
says, but i can clean it, since you caught it—they gather up the fishing equipment; we need to put this in your pack—natalia looks; i'm
not sure i have room—she lifts it over her shoulders, and nadine
puts the fishing rod in her pack, i'll carry the creel—i thought you
didn't like the smell. i didn't used to; i've gotten used to it. we'll
leave the fish in some water, walker says.

i wish we could catch salmon here, celia says, as they walk down
the trail; where will you go to school? i don't know, nadine says; i
haven't decided yet. what kind of doctor will you be? i could do almost anything—and maybe go to another country—i don't know
much about medicine, celia says; then, you might be living far away?

where the trail forks through the woods, only as far as these
train lines run. i'll come and visit you—anastasia holds her mother

in her arms, before the train pulls away; on the track to a city where robert worked, laying down wires that light the landscape, the train, as it pulls away on the track, and anastasia closes the blind to sleep, sitting next to rebecca—i wish she could come for a visit, too—but she's older, rebecca says, and now that father is gone, she doesn't go out as much—at least you live here and can take care of her—sometimes, anastasia says, i'm sorry that i moved away—you should take the train home more often—if i could get away from school—but you don't have to teach at all.

a track that snakes between two cities, like the trail where nadine and natalia walk, reading a diary aloud—i won't walk across—nadine stops at the log bridge—walker looks at the plank, then you can jump across—i'm going to get wet. natalia rolls her pants up and steps on the wood, it's not so bad, as her foot sinks into the mud; stepping on a clump of dry grass, she shakes her foot in the water, look—i don't want to go across—then how will we get back? nadine looks up and down the creek; shakes her head, and leaps. my foot is stuck in this muck—rinse it off—walker lifts celia over, before stepping across; you didn't even get wet—are we almost at the bottom? there's that cabin in the woods—nadine shakes a rock from her shoe, are your feet wet—no—then let's keep walking, walker says—yes. walker, natalia, celia and nadine, carrying their packs and fishing rods, almost at the bottom of the trail; a candle in the window of a cabin where america once stood, singing a song to herself—natalia picks up a piece of wood; we should build another campfire tonight, before we go back—as the trail behind them disappears, walker—anastasia says; this is where we will live—the car snakes through the woods and celia looks out, at the mountains and trees; when i come back—from across the ocean; a harbor, boats; nadine walks down the pavement; can you see the tent? there—nadine points, we're almost home now—yes—

anastasia standing on the trail, holding a hat in her hand as natalia splashes water on her face; rain splashing on the sidewalk where natalia looks, staring through the windowpane; a man on the street, haven't i seen you before; drinking a bottle of coke, shared demise, celia and walker, after anastasia is gone, a man sitting at a table, looking at natalia, a glance to someone or some-place far off, in the meadow where anastasia stands alone—reid, wearing an apron, as natalia waits and heath makes no remark; then, are you interested in him—i loaned him anastasia's diaries, natalia says; he likes reading about the past. they walk across the street, he's coming to our performance next week; erika sighs as they walk away; on the street corner, reid watches natalia—

waiting, until a man's name is cast in stone; a man made of brass carrying the weight of the world on his shoulders; one day, a woman standing in the meadow will turn to find herself all alone; rebecca opens the door to the house; sitting on the porch swing, anastasia takes off her boots; on a track that carries them to where anastasia lives, rebecca steps down from the train and looks at the fields, in patches of green, where do you go fishing? anastasia points, a patch of trees; does robert come with you? no—i'm glad that you are getting married, i would hate to see you living here alone—a man in the meadow who stares up at the sky, celia and walker, sitting in the church pew; i don't think we should come here—; once we are married, walker says, we don't need to come back—across the meadow, through the mountains and trees, wind blowing shutters against the wall, curtains carried by the breeze in natalia's apartment; walking across the floor; erika asks reid, you work in the coffee shop? yes—and you don't go to school—no. we need to go, erika says, we're performing in two hours—

a woman raising arms to the sky; america, shaking the snow from her cap and holding walker's hand, a boy that she gives birth to in the confines of a room; across the ocean, a man wearing a uniform—walker—america says, after his father; and anastasia, who went running through the woods—anastasia holds walker in her arms, his father should be here with you—we shouldn't, robert says, have let them go out alone—but you told me not to wait, america says, for a man—we wanted to get married, america says, even before he left—

carried like a grain of sand in glass; a hatpin, a pearl that anastasia finds, walking on the beach; walker says to america, i can have the pearl set, and send the ring back to you, in a letter—won't it get lost—and a picture, walker says; america folds the letter in her hand; anastasia says, soon, he'll come back—a candle in the window, reflecting against the glass; but i wouldn't wait, you could marry someone here—; america stands from her chair and raises the blinds, you almost didn't get married, aunt rebecca told me—but robert and i were married before you were born. then, america says, i will have walker's child, even if he doesn't come back—a ring that is placed, string or twine connecting tides to the moon, a thread of silver that natalia picks up, a pearl that natalia finds, and letters in a case, sent across the ocean, across the waves, a bottle carrying a message, a wedding ring, from a pearl on a hatpin that anastasia finds, walking on the beach—

one day, a woman will walk down a hillside carrying flowers, gazing into the sky at a star that falls; a woman giving birth to a boy, his voice when it is heard; anastasia and rebecca, wrapping walker in a blanket, handing him to america; anastasia looks out the window and rebecca asks, what will america name him? walker, anastasia says; after the father, who is gone? a ring on her finger; he will come back—on a starry night, the full moon above—someone worried and wondering, calling out his name—walker? rebecca asks; and after anastasia, america says, because she goes walking through the woods; rebecca looks out the window as she stands in america's room; what if he doesn't come back? then at least i'll have his son, walker, america says; a man in the meadow, never questioning her words—

a pearl that walker sends to america, across the ocean, string or twine in the folds of a letter that anastasia reads; rebecca closes the blinds; america should be getting some sleep—walker, as he steps away from america and she watches the train pull away, closing her eyes to sleep; anastasia, who carries walker up a dirt trail and through the meadow, to the place where she once walked as a girl—walker, wearing a pair of overalls, patting the dirt with his hands until, at the sound of thunder and rain, there you stand beneath the window watching natalia step out the door; my sister, natalia says to reid; reid—natalia says to nadine, he's reading anastasia's diaries—and he's coming with us, to hear the performance tonight—walking up the stairs, in a white dress and black shoes, there he is, erika says, the one in the cafe again—

nadine and reid sit in the audience, eyes focused on the podium where natalia and erika stand; don't faint, heath says; a performance that is about to begin, across the street where anastasia looks out the window, i'm sure that walker will come back—is that a letter from him? america takes the ring; a pearl that america places on her finger—a silver tide connected to the moon, after walker is born; running through the woods, building a sand castle, sticks and weeds, by the side of the stream, until anastasia shades her eyes against the setting sun, walker, it's time to go home.

america folds her chair; i caught two fish, america says as she walks down the trail, and robert arrives on the dirt road that carries them past houses and trees; here is where we will live, walker says, wearing a uniform; a house beside the ocean where america waits, holding the hand of a boy; here is where we will stay—in a small town; america says, he will be a doctor—

i could live in another country, nadine says, someplace far away—a place in the hills beyond—reid asks nadine, how many years of medical school do you have left? i haven't started yet—but i've saved enough money, at least to begin—are you nervous, heath asks natalia; yes—

a gown sewn in the confines of a room; celia's mother lays the dress on her bed, a white gown with lace; but don't make a train, celia says, i won't walk down an aisle carrying flowers; a dress that flows out behind her; anastasia turns—walker places anastasia's picture on his desk; one night, walker says, she just fell asleep—laying wires across the land; america and walker—my father, walker says to celia, came back to this county, after the war—after i was born—

celia looks at the fabric; try it on, her mother says, turning up the hem; but make it so i can walk in it—down an aisle wearing dark shoes; walker says, now that we are married, we don't have to come back, as the car pulls away; america dries her tears, shaking out her handkerchief to wave, as walker and celia drive through the woods, here is where we will stay—a house that is built, sticks and weeds, away from the boarding school where anastasia taught;

the place where america and walker arrive, after a house is built; here is where you will sleep, celia says; at the turning of a page, the clapping of hands that hold a hat, or thunder sounding from above, a girl growing beneath celia's hand as they walk up a trail; america and walker, sitting beside a pond, america puts a worm on a hook and throws her line into the water as walker says, i will walk up the trail; are you sure you don't want to come? walker shakes his head, no—then, i will come with you, celia says—to the place where walker will fish; then celia walks back down the trail alone, to america and walker, fishing, near the tent; are you sure, america asks, that you should walk so fast—celia, holding her hand to the heart of a girl, before she is born—walker never bothered me, america says; we'll come with you now—we don't have to wait until sunset—walker, casting his line into a stream, wearing waders as celia, walker and america wait, until they hear the sound of footsteps that echo; no one caught anything, celia says; we'll have to fix sandwiches—as they walk down the trail, before a girl is born—

in the confines of a room, white walls and a wood floor, and celia takes walker's hand; natalia's voice when it is heard, above the wail of a siren screaming, walking down an aisle, at a podium, or on the bank of a stream, a starry night surrounding her, as the performance is about to begin, in a church, in the wings, walker, celia, reid, and nadine, the woman in the director's chair, anastasia's eyes focused on the podium, shatter of glass, and gazing up at the moon or to the sky beyond the fields and trees, natalia and reid walk down the street, under the rain as though on a trail where walker picks natalia up to carry her in his arms; carrying a fishing rod and creel, walking down the trail to the pond below; he takes two fish from his creel and rinses them in the pond; howdy, campers—howdy, stranger—america lowers dark glasses from her eyes and walker stands from his chair; did you catch any fish—just one—, walker says; we caught three—america folds her chair—i can carry that for you—walker carries natalia to the other side of the pond, where celia waits by the tent, did you go hiking?

natalia waded into the water, i set her down by the stream—and she didn't cry to come back? running her fingers and toes through the grass, falling asleep by the pond, as america pulls in the line with her hand, a fish jumping in the water—look, walker says to natalia—america lands the fish on the bank; taking it off the hook, walker hits it hard, on the head, and natalia starts to cry—look, walker says to natalia, your grandmother caught a fish—we can cook it for dinner—natalia stares at the stars in the sky; celia holds her in her lap and walker throws the fish over the fire; only enough for a meal—celia feeds a piece of bread to natalia and walker stands in his waders, looking at shadows of the hills beyond; the woman and man sitting, after the sun has gone down; celia picks up natalia, i'm going to put her to bed—america, walker and natalia's father sit by the fire, america stirring the coals until they are lit; did we bring marshmallows? walker takes some from a bag, and natalia's father strips the bark from a stick; natalia would like one, america says, as celia emerges from the tent; she's asleep—a child that is growing, beneath celia's hand—

where did she come from? natalia asks; under a canopy, under the moon; celia wraps nadine in a blanket to carry her on the trail; walker, taking natalia's hand, i'll take natalia with me, unless she wants to go hiking—we'll go fishing—natalia picks up a stick; hiking with walker up the trail, carry me across—walker picks her up and carries her on his shoulders, across a marsh or a brook in the meadow, i'm getting tired—and natalia falls asleep in the grass where walker sets her down; pulling on his waders and tying a fly on the line, walker wades into the stream, casting his line into the water and natalia hears the whistling, as he whips the line up from the water and back into the stream; a woman in a long dress as natalia closes her eyes to sleep, the sound of the fly rod above the noise of the stream, running, a woman wearing a hat as walker turns to look—natalia—it's time to go home—lifting natalia onto his shoulders, carrying his fishing rod in one hand, the noise of his footsteps echoing against the cliff walls that surround him, the ground soft beneath his feet as he carries natalia, asleep on his back, to the meadow where the tent is pitched, and celia and nadine wait, for the sound of footsteps, or thunder echoing overhead as it starts to rain, and celia carries nadine inside; walker puts natalia down beside nadine, until the sun comes out and celia takes a broom to sweep water from the canvas floor, while walker sets nadine outside; have you seen eleanor clay? celia asks; yes—natalia brings nadine's doll from the tent—a veritable army of men, celia seems, sweeping the water up and away, into the clear morning light—

in a church, in the wings, natalia raising her arms to the sky, heath, as he tunes his violin and erika sings, under the stained glass, under the moon as it begins to rain by the pond, on the old people, fishing, from the director's chairs—where have they gone? natalia asks when she comes home; walker, sitting at the table, arms folded across his chest; does he begin to cry—at the sight of a woman that is fading, a woman who lifts her skirt to walk through the weeds, one who is sitting and fishing still, as walker approaches the pond, is this woman one and the same as the woman wearing dark glasses to shield her eyes from the sun; under a canopy as celia makes her bed and the sun starts to rise, natalia—

heath calling from the sidewalk as she lies in bed; i didn't hear you—you're already late—she sits at a table with reid, shared demise—walker taking celia's hand; across a table, wearing dark glasses, still as impenetrable as the moon—

eyes focused on her, in a church, in the wings, america as she stands by the stream lowering dark glasses from her eyes, does she turn around to see, natalia standing there and shivering in the mist; walker and nadine; anastasia takes out a handkerchief to wave, walking away, does she have something to say, something to tell walker now, as he stands alone fishing, or walking down the trail past the old people, sitting still and fishing, from the director's chairs as the performance is about to begin, as though in a dream, natalia stands at the podium, let me carry you across, the words of a man seldom spoken, a sight unseen, the sound of two notes when they are heard, then three, strains of notes in the night, crossed by harmonies, a bridge, span of wires, a discordant sound as natalia writes and heath picks up his violin, in a church, in the wings, a man in a black robe kneeling down to pray, under the shatter of stained glass where reid waits, anastasia, writing with a feather pen, words written at a time that has not been forgotten, in a diary, and letters in a case, under lock and key until natalia and nadine read, a man in a cafe wearing a red shirt and black flannel pants, under the sight of two women as he begins to read anastasia's diary, words from another time, not so long ago, as natalia bathes her toes in the stream and walker approaches the old man and woman, fishing from the director's chairs as the sun starts to go down and walker, natalia, and nadine appear on the trail, were you lost? or only hiding from the light as it fell from above, a stream of light, a cone, like the train of a woman's dress when she walks down an aisle; i won't walk down an aisle in a white gown; marry me or carry my child; does it make a difference now, who wrote these notes across a line, words from a feather pen as reid closes the book, on a table, beneath the moonlight as it falls to the sidewalk, walker sees the sight of a woman fading, wearing a long dress in a dark room, two candles framing the window where anastasia sits, her face in the glass, someone worried and wondering, calling out a name—

a man in a black robe, kneeling down to pray beneath anastasia's gaze, someone walking down an aisle wearing white shoes, black pants and a white shirt, a black jacket and she looks as heath raises his violin and erika stands in a black dress, singing the first note of a melody as walker, celia, nadine and reid wait, for the sounds before they are heard—

is there something of the night, dear reader, something about the way stars shine in the middle of winter, before two girls shake snow from the leaves of a tree, still shaking, the people fishing from the director's chairs, does walker sit down and cry, a hand across his face as he glances to the moon, brushing the tears away; there is no woman in a long flowing gown; fishing from the director's chairs, that will be walker, one day; the piece as it begins on violin and erika sings, a woman in a black dress, gold band around her neck, eyes of an audience focused, an opera glass, is it america; is this woman someone we can, if we lower glasses from our eyes, see sitting at a table or conducting an orchestra, where natalia stands in a church while reid watches the snow fall, as a chorus of angels with wings that billow in the wind, on a starry night, under the full moon; natalia, opening the church door, pulling at the brass handle and walking to where candles are lit, reflected in the glass, where anastasia sits, writing in her diary; had she thrown away the key—

walking down an aisle in a white gown, celia turns, looking at the mountains around her she says to nadine, do you want to climb that one? as natalia reads the words of anastasia's diary, her picture on the piano, eyes focused on natalia as she is writing, or conducting an orchestra as the piece begins in a church, walker closes his eyes to see the sight of a woman raising her arms to the sky, flowers thrown over a banister—

a name cast in stone, anastasia where she lies as though asleep, beside the church where she grew up, beside robert, a stone that bears their names; a chorus of women's voices singing, satin sleeves billowing in the wind that blows and scatters leaves across the sidewalk, pulling hair like a river current, at a cool and tranquil time, when a woman pulled off her boots and long skirts to bathe; natalia, beneath anastasia's gaze as the orchestra plays, anastasia and walker, reid, two dancers carried on the wind, across the sidewalk to the beach where reid and natalia walk across the sand, as waves rise and recede, a castle, with turrets, a moat, a door, look— anastasia shakes out her handkerchief to wave, and nadine sails away, to a house beside a market place, sticks and weeds, where wind blows through the trees, blowing sand across the doorstep and into the house where nadine lives in the summer, across the ocean, this is where i will live, nadine thinks, as she walks to her house; this is where i will stay, as the tide comes in and recedes, wind blowing through the door and down the aisle, as though to carry her to another place, not so fraught with memory even as the past disappears, underneath these wheels, from hawkes point to north point, as the orchestra plays, words seldom spoken by a man who stands at a pulpit wearing a black robe, underneath the stained glass, reid listens to the strains of notes on heath's violin and erika as she sings, at the clang of a church bell, walker and celia listen, does a man in a black robe walk away; a woman conducting the orchestra, listening as though to the running of a stream, it is anastasia, growing beneath the confines of anastasia's skirt, america, an old woman before she is born; one day, a girl wearing a dress and carrying a doll to hike up a mountainside will move to another place; sitting in a church and listening to the orchestra, walker takes a handkerchief to wipe his eyes, mere pinpoints of light focused on natalia, does anastasia shade her eyes against the spotlight where the orchestra members sit; is the woman wearing dark glasses someone we can, if we shade our eyes, see sitting beside natalia, listening from the director's chair as though beside a pond; leaves blowing across the churchyard where celia and walker place flowers on the stone that bears anastasia's and robert's names; did a wind come to carry them across this mountain meadow, to where nadine lives beside an ocean, before going back to school; a hatpin, a pearl, washed up on the beach where natalia and reid wait for a message as though sent in a bottle; crash of ocean waves against the shore, a melody, wind in the trees, blowing through the city where traffic flows like a river, a train whistle wailing, as america waves and steam disappears into the air, like tears natalia brushed from her eyes as a girl; eyes focused on the orchestra, gold of an opera glass, round like the gold band on a woman's hand; i won't walk down an aisle wearing a white gown, carrying flowers in the folds of an apron, a bundle, a girl; someday, a woman walking down an aisle will wear black pants and a white shirt, as a piece begins and a man sits, listening to erika as she sings a melody played by violins, and a man lights a candle, as though to pray for the time when a woman would walk down an aisle wearing a white gown, to where a man waited, a ring around her finger, string or twine, cast in stone; flowers thrown across the stage, a woman stepping over petals as though across the stream where she once stood fishing, wearing a hat and carrying a walking stick, does a man in the meadow understand, that one day the eyes of a woman from a picture will stare with pinpoint focus on a girl; standing at the podium, natalia closes her eyes to see, something carried to her like a grain of sand in her palm, a pearl, a world seen as though from hawkes point to north point, carried smooth as a sailing ship to a place she cannot see yet, nor begin to understand; is the woman still sitting, fishing from the director's chair, someone we can see, like the thoughts of another time, written by a woman with a feather pen; reid puts his book down, as anastasia smoothes the wrinkles from her skirt, natalia, walking between the pews, where reid sits, a bundle of flowers in her arms, clack of quick heels across white tiles, snap of a violin case as heath turns to walk away, does someone look for natalia now; or is it only the sound of notes flowing like a river, as though beneath the moon that connects tides to this beach where natalia and reid walk; carry me across—across the tides, a glance falls from a face as a hand across the moon; petals scattered across a stage like leaves where the orchestra members walk, out the door and across the lawn where leaves blow in the wind; traffic that sounds like a stream, whistle of a train as it is leaving; nadine picks up her suitcase as anastasia shakes out her handkerchief to wave; drops of rain streaking the window glass as nadine is carried, like a grain of sand in an hourglass, across the ocean, to a time not so fraught with memories, fragmented by dreams; natalia, staring at the stained glass, listening to notes as they fall, eyes focused as though from a picture in a frame; a voice silent and still until there you stand, listening, as nadine is carried across the sky, beyond the church where celia and walker walk down the aisle, does the carpet sink beneath their feet as they pull at the brass door, as reid, natalia, nadine, celia and walker walk down the stairs and across the lawn, where leaves blow across the aisle and down the street, where traffic flows by in a stream—

walker shades his eyes against the sun to see the old people; does the woman take off her visor, the glasses from her eyes, as walker approaches; behind him, natalia and nadine; does he begin to understand a man walking down a hillside carrying a bundle of flowers, or a girl; that one day, the thoughts of a man will fade; the old man and woman as they are sitting, still, sipping at their tea and fishing from the director's chairs; natalia—anastasia turns, as though to follow her through the woods; does she hold one hand on her hat, to keep it from coming off; a conversation, that voice that surrounds us, coming from a place in the blackness never seen; wind scattering snowflakes like leaves, falling onto stained glass, streaking the colored glass like rain; erika, by the pond where the old man and woman are sitting, does a wind blow across the ocean to carry them away; is there something in the night, dear reader, something of the silence in the trees, as walker shakes a stone from his shoe, and someone tears the dirt away; a casket made of wood, a woman who once went wandering through the woods, wearing a long dress or her father's trousers, fishing by the side of the stream; natalia stands from beneath the canopy where rain has started to fall on america's name, cast in stone; america, lying beside walker, beneath the grass, flowers sitting in a vase, sitting still above america's name as walker, celia, natalia and nadine walk down a gravel path, a car that goes past hawkes point to north point, to a time no one can remember; a place no one has seen—a grain of sand in a glass, falling; two girls standing beside the pond; the woman in the director's chair, does she have something to say, something to tell them now, as natalia stands fishing by the side of the stream; can she see america, if she looks—through an opera glass to the hills that surround her, the stars that float as though carried on the wind, to the place nadine lives, walking to a market place, dresses of brightly woven cloth, clay pots and tables where dust flies up like leaves, particles glowing beneath the sun, under a full moon, on a night in winter as the snow begins to fall, natalia and reid close the shutters; as though a ring around a finger, the gold of the moon reflected off the ocean, connecting tides to this beach where wind rattles the leaves of palms, like the sound of maracas shaking, a chorus of women, notes running like the stream where walker stands, under a cloudy sky, drops of rain falling over the river bank, causing the river to swell and flow, as celia brushes tears from her eyes, sweeping dirt from the tent, particles of dust that rise through the air, reflecting the sun like the gold of a ring, the moonlight carried by ocean waves that splash against this shore, where america once swam, a beach ball hovering as though a grain of sand that falls in a glass, even as we speak, dear reader, across a point in time, natalia walks under a spotlight, and reid listens, as though to words cast in a diary with a feather pen, as rain falls, in streaks of gold beneath the moon that never questions this world, a woman singing as though in a long flowing gown, as though she has something to say, dear reader, something to tell us now, as the old man and woman move their chairs around the pond, walker, casting his line into the stream, in the meadow that connects the moon to the forest, a place where wind kicks up dust like leaves, on a gravel road beneath palm trees that rattle in the wind, maracas shaking, then timpani, as heath picks up his violin, connecting tides to the moon, white foam of ocean waves that wash over the sand, as though carrying a message to nadine, to where the sun reflects off the water and into walker's eyes, by the stream as celia waits, looking to the valley below, a woman in a long skirt gathering flowers, will they put these in a vase before the sun starts to go down, and natalia closes the blinds; anastasia takes out a handkerchief to wave as she lifts her skirts to wade through the stream, at the sound of a train whistle wailing, a locomotive, steam, rising to form clouds above the river, where walker holds one hand to his hat to keep it from coming off; natalia, nadine—walking to the meadow where celia reads a book and the tent is pitched; a man who reads a diary; a letter; nadine, across the ocean from where the letter is sent, ink across a page carrying words, like wind carrying stars or grains of sand to a churchyard, leaves that blow against stained glass, impenetrable as a bottle where this message sits, carried to you and the woman fishing from the director's chair; a boy wearing overalls, taking diaries from the trunk where they sit, blowing dust from the covers, particles that land on a pink dress anastasia wore as the words were written, a page deciphered by the woman wearing dark glasses, a veil across her face, a woman on a dusty street, palms rattling in the wind, no traffic flowing as nadine walks home, the mail as it is carried, a medical book, from hawkes point to north point, across the meadow to where walker stands fishing, the old woman in the director's chair, could she be one and the same as the woman sitting, taking pins from her hair, pulled by the current of the stream where she sits bathing, still bathing, does she see the sight of a woman fading, wondering at the hair that spills out beneath a straw hat as you hold it with one hand, to keep it from coming off. is there something of the night in the meadow, something of the stars as wind blows, shaking leaves from trees, where a woman wears bright colored cloth like white lace, lifting a bundle tied into white cloth onto her head, holding a hand to the bundle, to keep it from coming off; it is i, in the meadow, it is you, taking my place, walking down a gravel road that cuts through tall grass, across the land where robert lies, beneath a stone that bears his name; anastasia, next to america; walker shades his eyes to see the old people sitting, wind blowing leaves, wafting into the air before falling against the current, carried through streets and to the ocean, to america, before the sun sets, and walker walks to where celia tends the fire, stirring the coals until they are lit—

a melody spanned by wires, anastasia writing with a feather pen, in the meadow, beside a rock as reid and natalia sit, reading anastasia's diary before they walk, further still, from the trail; a man who looks, were they lost?

beneath a fragment of the moon, someone worried and wondering, calling out a name.

biographical note

America Hart is the director of the MA Creative Writing Program at London Metropolitan University. Her work has appeared in journals and publications such as *Black Ice*, *Sniper Logic*, *Blackbox Manifold*, *Shearsman Magazine*, *Stride Magazine*, and the *Journal of African Cultural Studies*. Her honors include a Rocky Mountain Women's Institute Fellowship and the Jovanovich Award from the University of Colorado. She has received research grants to conduct fieldwork in Jamaica, Zimbabwe, and Ghana. Born and raised in Colorado, America lived in Boston and New York City before moving to London, where she lives with her partner, Seraphin.